SIDE LAUNCH

SIDE LAUNCH

A Novel

Laurie Fullerton

Copyright ©2025, Laurie Fullerton

ISBN Paperback: 979-8-9987373-0-5

For information, please contact:
Laurie Fullerton
Hantsport Press
hantsportpress@gmail.com

Cover design by Nick Kent.
Cover photo ©2022 by Linda Cunningham Photography.

ACKNOWLEDGMENTS

The author would like to thank the wonderful Stephen Morrison for his editorial expertise, incredible feedback, time, and encouragement. Additional thanks to Elizabeth Barrett for her critique and Susan Lovett for edits. Special thanks to readers and helpful friends Erin Trahan, David Roper, Meghan McCloskey, Humphrey Gardner and Theresa Milewski.

The author would also like to thank my mother Carol Fullerton for her encouragement as well as Pam Fullerton, Deborah Johnson, Greta Hertel, Gwen Hertel, David Johnson and the extended Upton clan.

CHAPTER ONE

Susannah Pierce was driving down a rural highway in Maine when she passed an exit sign that said To Ossonet Historic District. She was not in a hurry, and she was a bit hungry. She made an abrupt decision to turn off the main road and follow the sign. She was pleased that as she traveled the road, she could see a glimpse of water in the distance.

It was late afternoon as she drove through the quiet town looking for the historic district. She passed a sign in front of a church that said Ham and Bean Supper Tonight. She parked and walked toward the church. She could smell the aroma of baked beans wafting from the open door and saw a woman walking toward it, a bit flushed, carrying a large beanpot. She could hear people inside offering help. It seems there were already pots of warm beans in the kitchen, and more were arriving with little time to spare before the Saturday night traditional supper started at six.

"Excuse me, can you tell me where the historic district is?" Susannah asked, feeling hungrier as she got a look at the vast pot of beans.

"There really ain't one, dearie," she said in a thick Maine accent, shaking her head. "Suppah stahts at six shahp and these have to stay wahm." She headed for the church kitchen. Susannah offered to help her carry the pot, but the woman was "quite capable, thank you very much."

"Do you mind if I look around inside for a minute?" Susannah asked.

"Fine by me," the woman said and hefted her large frame and

heavy beanpot over toward a group of women standing around an industrial-size kitchen.

It was a simple parish hall with wooden floors and a small stage at the end of it, likely used for an old-fashioned Christmas pageant. There was nothing much else in the hall but a dilapidated, broken-down piano in the corner. She heard the women's banter in the kitchen and considered asking them about the age of the piano when she noticed a glass casing nearby. There was a preserved letter inside. It read:

On June 22, 1947, the 70-foot schooner *Katrina M* was launched at the Benjamin Dodd shipyard. This marks the last time on record that our congregation will ring our cherished Paul Revere church bell to herald the launching of a schooner. Our whole town and congregation are saddened that shipbuilding in Ossonet ends on this day.

It was signed by the Reverend Howard Aldrich, Ossonet, Maine, 1947.

Susannah liked history and prided herself on her experiences overseas working and living with an anthropologist. There was something about this town that stirred up her urge for further study and observation. To add to her curiosity, Susannah was returning from a newspaper conference in Boston. She had been heading to Clydebank, the small coastal city not too far from Ossonet where she now worked and lived. The conference was required for her job at the *Clydebank News*, but one short seminar on the task of news gathering—or finding stories—felt anthropological in nature to her. The lecturer had suggested a good news gatherer should follow their instincts and wait around for a story to emerge, just as an anthropologist must observe and wait.

She did not have to wait long. She was looking up at the steeple when four men pulled up in front of the church in a pickup truck.

"Going to the ham and bean suppah tonight?" one of them asked her as he tipped his hat to her and walked into the parish hall.

The man who spoke to her was tall, wearing wire-rimmed spectacles, a blue flat cap, and work pants. A few minutes later, the men came out with the old piano. They were carrying it toward the pickup truck.

"The church asked us to get rid of this old thing, but it's going out in style," the tall man said to her.

"How's that?" she answered, catching on to his attempts at friendly banter.

"We are having a piano-burning party tonight!" he said.

One of the other men said, "Heads up! Dodd!" They needed his attention so they could give the piano one more heave onto the truck. The men drove off in the direction of the waterfront. She watched them turn towards some derelict buildings, and then they were gone.

She decided to walk from the church up a small hill to a country store. It turned out they still sold the newspaper she was working for. She bought the most recent edition of her newspaper, as well as a whoopie pie and a cup of coffee, and tucked the paper under her arm. She walked toward the waterfront, hands full, sipping her coffee, taking a bite of the whoopie pie, then sat clumsily down on a nearby bench.

As she ate, she noticed the boats were nearly aground, so she figured the tide was "goin'," not "comin'," as Mainers say. Yet, before long she could see quite clearly from the ripples and movement of the water that the tide was "comin'." The grounded boats seemed to come to life as the tide came in and started to move as they increasingly had water beneath them to float again. Soon enough, they began to bob up and down on their moorings. She was surprised to see not only how quickly the tide rushed in, but how deep the area around the waterfront was as it formed a tidal basin complete with a small whirlpool at the center of it. Susannah knew enough to assume that in a deep river port like this one filled with boats, one could go from here at high tide, through the basin, past the distant shore, and ultimately out farther into the vast Gulf of Maine and North Atlantic.

As she was eating her hockey puck-shaped chocolate cake and white frosting treat, it had at first baffled her that they were called "pies." Like many things about Maine, there was a maritime explanation. When working fishermen and lobstermen needed sustenance while out on the ocean, they ate homemade "hand pie" which was a mince, turkey, or meat pie that could be eaten with one hand while still operating a boat without the ingredients spilling out. The whoopie pie remains an intact dessert that can be consumed while operating a boat or a vehicle. This humble hand pie evolved into an iconic Maine road food, and Mainers could not resist them.

She looked across the bay and noticed a derelict railroad bridge and abandoned railway tracks that ran along the shore. The old tracks continued around a small peninsula and out of sight. She started walking in that direction and found a plaque that read "Between 1740 and 1947, over 5,000 schooners were built in Ossonet. During the 20th century, Ossonet schooners were known as 'the gold standard of North American shipbuilding.'" In reading it she realized the plaque was at the center of the historic district, but from what she could tell, it was all that was left of the town's history.

She continued toward the shore and passed through what seemed like a junkyard. She was surprised to find a little road at the end of it. She crossed a small creek bridge. At its end was a house on the water and what looked like an old boatyard with a large barn at the river's edge.

The brown clapboard house was accessible by a narrow road that crossed the creek and was situated on a naturally formed marsh island, surrounded by wetlands on three sides and a river flowing past it. The land around the house had been fortified and heightened by hundreds of years of human habitation with distinct mounds and dips indicating where countless shipwrights may have walked. The area around the house had well-worn footpaths, and there were some old machines and several woodsheds filled with cut wood. There was a sawmill and piles of logs resting near it, but the mill looked unused and was covered with pine needles. It seemed the whole place was decomposing under the weight of hundreds of years of use that had formed mounds and grassy knolls and unusual terrain across the property and was then left to dry out with lack of use and become covered with bracken, brambles and a lot of discarded junk.

The house itself, situated on the highest point on the island marsh, looked abandoned, but she had learned since moving to Maine that the most ramshackle houses were not always empty of life. She looked for an eggs for sale sign, which was one sure way of letting a passerby know that a house was far from deserted. Outside the door, she saw a plaque next to a large ship's bell that said Built for Amos Dodd, 1825. She didn't dare ring the bell as she was trying to be an observer. Out of courtesy, she knocked quietly, but no one answered.

She heard a sound in the nearby barn—which was built on stilts along the water's edge—and headed toward its open door. She felt an immediate cooling breeze once she stepped inside. The floor was swept clean, and it smelled like linseed oil. Fresh sawdust, reflected in a beam of sunlight from the side door, led her eye toward the barn wall filled with antique tools. There was a painted sign just inside the door that said Wood for Sale. Another sign of life. She took a quick picture and turned to leave when someone spoke to her from the loft.

"You a real estate agent?" a man asked from the top of the stairs just after her camera clicked.

"No. Hi. I, um, I think I am trespassing," she said apologetically.

"Ya think?" he asked with a hint of sarcasm. She looked up and realized it was the tall man she had just seen at the church.

"Oh, hi!" she said sheepishly. "I saw you earlier."

"Do I know you?" he asked and pushed his spectacles up closer to his face.

He looked taller and broader shouldered than when she had seen him at the church. His long legs cast a shadow down the loft steps, making them seem even longer now as he braced against the wall at the top of the stairway. His arms were crossed in front of him.

"Sorry, I am actually looking for the historic district," she fumbled. "For a minute there I thought I had found it."

"I guess you could call me historic," he said. She felt it was an invitation to ask a few more questions.

"Do you live here?" she asked.

"Ayuh, I live here. In my house, I mean, yeah." He gestured toward the house. "Well, it is really Amos Dodd's house, but he hasn't lived here for quite a while."

"About 200 years give or take?" she ventured.

"Got that right!" he said.

She looked along the wall of the barn going up the loft stairs and noticed at least thirty mounted, carved mahogany wooden half-hull or half-ship models, which was only one half of a boat's hull without rigging or other fixtures. She recognized them to be nautical art, something you might see over a mantelpiece or on the wall at a seafood restaurant. Here in the barn, they all had a polished luster to them, and they were affixed with a small brass mount with the name and year a ship was built engraved into the brass. From what she could read, it seemed many were from the early 1900s.

"Where did you get all of these beautiful pieces of nautical art?" she asked, gesturing toward all the half-hull models.

"Art?" He sounded confused. "Why, you wanna buy one?"

"No, I don't have any room in my small apartment in Clydebank," she revealed. "There is hardly room for me to turn around in it, much less hang something. But they are beautiful."

He started coming down the stairs from the loft and reached for one of the half models she was admiring. "You live in Clydebank. Are you sure you're not a realtor?" He handed her the model. It was heavy and smooth. She felt like an anthropologist again, like she was touching an artifact or something sacred to a tribe.

"Yes and no to answer your question. To be honest, I stopped here and have been trying to find the historic district, if there is one," she said as if it was vitally important that she find it. "I'm Susannah."

"If you want to find your historic district, it's in your hands. You are holding what's left." His tone was a bit resigned. "This is the half-hull of the Katrina M," he said, and she recognized the name from the encased letter at the church.

"The last one built here?" she asked.

"Ayuh," he said in a sullen tone. Then, "I'm Owen Dodd, by the way," but it was spoken less as an introduction and more with a heavy sigh.

The large collection of half-hull models in the barn was, in fact, a daily reminder to Owen Dodd that a way of life that he was born to live was gone for good. Owen, who was now thirty-four, had held onto his dream of being a master shipwright and building a vessel as large as his ancestor's had. He had spent much of his life in this loft surrounded by all the tools needed to build a schooner. He had taught himself the techniques for using the tools by reading and rereading every book left up in the loft since the 1940s. He took notes from these books, especially if Ossonet was mentioned, as it often was. He had pored over photographs he found of Ossonet's glory days of shipbuilding.

He went on about the ship models to this curious stranger. He told her half-hulls are tools for any shipwright in the days before a schooner was built, before computers. They are the wooden model or prototype needed as a first step before construction. Since thousands of schooners were built in Ossonet since the 1700s, there were at one time an endless supply of beautiful Ossonet half-hull models around town. Over time, there were fewer to be found. What remained in town ended up hanging in barns like Owen's or in living rooms in Ossonet.

Eventually most of them were given away to antique dealers or home furnishing shops.

"So, no one here is doing any shipbuilding now?" she ventured, handing the model back to him.

It was a loaded, complicated question, and Owen seemed reluctant to talk about it with this attractive, yet nosy, stranger. A fresh pretty face standing in his barn was a sharp reminder of his fading hopes that he could hold onto the family's shipyard property. He hoped he could one day find a customer who wanted to pay him to build an Ossonet schooner. He was now in his mid-thirties and still waiting, as Owen did not fit into any modern-day occupation and was awkward in and around society. But in temperament and personality, he was perfectly suited to be an 18th century shipwright. By honoring the trade and traditions that ran through his family line for generations, he had unknowingly adopted and preserved some of the cultural ticks, quirks, and traits that set him apart in modern terms. This tall, lanky, Mainer seemed burdened with a mindset that he must build large schooners, and although no one was telling him he had to, try as he might, he was obsessed with this one goal.

"If you are so interested, why don't you come by the piano-burning party tonight?"

"OK, maybe I will." As she was leaving, she noticed that he had green eyes. She had not seen that color very often and it drew her in more than she wanted to admit.

He had described the party as being "on the outskirts of town," and Susannah had been driving around, but it was now dark. Finally, she passed the same trucks she had seen earlier parked in front of the sheds now lined up right near a farm. She could smell woodsmoke and spotted a small group standing in a field. So, this was a piano burning party?

She walked up to a circle of mostly men standing with beers in their hands. They wore wool vests and tan Carhartt jeans with rigging knives on their belts. Although there was no wooden shipbuilding going on anymore, they seemed to dress as if there were. There were a couple of women there too, and one of them waved hello to her from across the fire. They looked to be about her age, somewhere in their early thirties. They were all watching the growing bonfire with the piano in the middle of it as it started to smolder. She joined the circle and felt the thrill of being in the tribe, even for a moment, and not just on the outside looking in.

The wind shifted, and the thickening smoke from the piano was now coming toward her. She stepped to one side to avoid the smoke, and in doing so practically bumped into a man named Seb. He had also abruptly moved away from the smoke, so they collided hard.

"I hate rabbits. Repeat after me," he said.

It was an odd thing to say, and she suddenly worried she had stumbled upon some kind of coven or a cult that she wanted no part of.

"I hate rabbits," he said again. "If you say 'I hate rabbits,' the smoke will stop blowing in your face."

Relieved, she said, "I hate rabbits!" and stepped slightly to the left.

The flames increased around the back of the piano. Suddenly a theatrical and colorfully dressed man wearing a long black coat and a top hat pushed through the group. She heard the crowd say, "Go, Owen!" He stood near the smoldering instrument, flexing his fingers like a true showman, preparing to play. As the flames grew, Owen Dodd placed his hands on the smoky keys and proceeded to play, quite poorly, the progression chords of a classic rock song. He quickly finished the second stanza as smoke surrounded him, and the flames got closer. He then ran his fingers across the keyboard in a final flourish as the keys were now burning and starting to grow too hot to touch.

He leapt away from the encroaching fire and dove back toward the circle, losing his balance. He slammed into Seb, who grabbed him and kept him from falling. He spun around as Seb hit at his coat and tried to get all the sparks off him. He finally collected himself and still steaming, said, "Seb, are you stealing my date?" He gave Seb a nudge.

"No," Seb laughed. "You are too hot to touch right now. Besides, I don't even know her name."

"This is Seb," Owen said to Susannah. Then he slapped his friend on the back and started dusting himself off. "This lady is a real estate agent named Susannah."

"Not." Susannah was a bit embarrassed. "I work as a reporter at the *Clydebank News*."

Seb looked intrigued and regarded her more closely, as if he couldn't see her that well.

Then, "As a reporter, does she know the whole story, Owen, besides you not being the piano man?" Seb asked. "Does she know who you are?"

"I think he said he is basically the historic district," she answered Seb.

"Historic district?" Seb said. "Twelve generations of Dodds built ships here in town. I guess you could say he is kind of a relic. We all are relics of the past," Seb said as he gestured around the circle.

"The sign to the historic district is misleading," Susannah said, referring to the highway turnoff. "I didn't know it was here in this field I would meet all of the ancient ruins."

"You have now," Seb nodded.

Owen then noticed his hair was singed, and he brushed more hot embers off his smoldering coat. "Problem is we museum pieces are not fireproof," Owen added. "Seb, can you get me a beer and a fire extinguisher?"

CHAPTER TWO

Susannah was staring out the window at the weekly assignment meeting in the dusty, dim conference room at the *Clydebank News*. Her editor, Bill King, was droning on about a large-scale municipal project that might finally clean up Clydebank harbor. Bill had been a newspaper reporter and editor most of his life. Now in his 50s, with greying hair and bifocals, and like many newsmen who have toiled their whole lives in local journalism, he often wore a tie and rumpled blue blazer to work. Bill was kind but firm when it came to seniority among the staff. Susannah was the lowest man, so to speak, on the totem pole and had yet to prove herself. He was reluctant to give her the best assignments, but he did see she had some potential to write and report. As usual during meetings, she was gazing out the window, and although there were two other reporters in the room, he picked her and asked, "Can you give me 500 words on the state of the proposed harbor cleanup and new sewage treatment facility—unless you have something else?"

Susannah was about to answer when her phone pinged, and she saw it was a text from Owen Dodd. It said, *I have a good story for you. Can you swing by?*

"I might have a good story out of Ossonet," she said to the room.

Susannah readjusted herself in the chair, pushing back her hair and sitting up straight. It was difficult as she had long legs and long arms, and at five foot ten inches wearing heels, her knees often got stuck underneath the desk. As she sat up, she shook the whole table and apologized to it and everyone in the room. As she did battle with the chair, the morning sun highlighting the natural blond streaks in her strawberry-blond hair, the men in the room were slightly amused by her loud fidgeting. She was of Scottish descent and had inherited the hair color of the Scots, which contrasted with her deep brown eyes and nicely rounded face. She had that slightly ruddy complexion that is also common in Scotland. If she had been paying attention, she might have realized that Bill and the other reporters in the room were not annoyed with her inattention but liked her presence at the newspaper office. They could tell, however, that she was restless and slightly bored. She always entered the room with a loud sigh and was always clumsy about how she sat down. She seemed to most of the staff to be a bit too exotic for Clydebank's slow pace. She was probably one of the most attractive women in their community, and single, but by Clydebank standards, she was a little intimidating. Besides, as most Mainers would agree, she was "from off island. From away," and that made it harder for her to adapt and be accepted.

She sat up straighter. "I may have something else for you. A possible story out of Ossonet. I may have to go there today. It is about some old-town traditions under threat, I think. It could be interesting." The town was within the same county as Clydebank, and Bill King was happy to get some coverage for one of the rural towns that they usually ignored.

"Okay," Bill agreed. "Go for it."

As she drove to Ossonet, she started thinking about anthropology. She had spent much of her post-college life traveling and then living in southeast Asia with a British anthropologist named Eric Strand. They met on a beach in the Philippines and spent far too long in a bungalow, mostly lounging around and swimming in the warm waters of the Philippine Sea before he had to begin his anthropological work in Laos and would take up residency there. When he invited her to come with him to his worksite in Laos, she grabbed at the opportunity.

Ossonet was the first place—in a long time—that held some interest to her and sparked a bit of motivation and comparison to that amazing anthropological work. Perhaps she just had something to prove, as he had sent her a copy of his most recent scholarly book to her parents' address around the same time she had stopped in Ossonet. Her parents had forwarded it to her Clydebank address, and although she did receive a thank you for her work, to her dismay, it was a "thanks to Susannah for support and encouragement." He did not even include her last name, so of course she could not receive even the slightest bit of credit for any of it.

She had initially convinced herself that she had a strictly academic interest in Owen Dodd, this thirty-four-year-old bachelor whose parents still lived in the same town. He had become the trustee of the abandoned Dodd house on the shipyard property sometime in his twenties, when his siblings had gone off to college and jobs. In the family's minds, the home and former shipyard was a living link to Ossonet's shipbuilding past, and it seemed natural that Owen wanted to live there. While a good newspaper person would report it as a couple of derelict Maine properties owned by old Yankee families, an anthropologist might see that to some it was sacred ground.

Susannah had been doing a bit of reading about schooners at the local library. The first genuine schooner on record was developed in or around 1713 and may have been adapted from a Dutch design. In Ossonet, Owen's ancestor had been there from the beginning, dating back to 1725, just six years after the first-ever schooner was documented. From before the Revolutionary War, during the Civil War, World War I, and even World War II, schooners by far were the most important North American ship in the nation. It is known that as shipbuilding evolved over the centuries, both Dodd's and Gregory's and the town itself were relevant in this industry with up to five trains a day coming and going from the shipyards with supplies, men and for trade. Schooners evolved into beautiful, fast, and sleek vessels, and the story goes that someone once remarked about one of the vessels under sail, "Oh, how she schoons!" and the name stuck. A schooner is a vessel with two or more masts, typically with the foremast smaller than the mainmast, and having gaff-rigged lower masts. The gaff means that some of the schooner's many sails are square on top, while the foremast sails are triangular. As the vessel evolved, Ossonet schooners were used for the coastal trade and for fishing, as on the Grand Banks off Newfoundland, and soon after 1800, the schooner caught the attention of shipwrights throughout Europe, Asia, and North and South America, who built versions of their own. The fore-and-after masts became popular all over the world. In the United States, where speed became a premium in the China trade and the California gold trade in the mid-nineteenth century, the schooner design was seen as the precursor to the old full rigged three-masted merchantman, resulting in the famous clipper ships and the Golden Age of Sail.

It may have been why Owen referred to himself as the historic district. He had the task of running a shipyard in an industry that had breathed its last breath in 1947. There wasn't a huge amount of work available. But he had kept working on small projects while sharing the techniques he had learned from history, oral traditions, and a kind of keen ability to think like an eighteenth-century shipwright. He read and reread every book he could find on shipbuilding, and he also spent time talking with old timers who once worked in either the Dodd or Gregory shipyards, as these were the two families who forged so much history in one town. Over the years, men like Owen had spent a lot of time on the old property across from Owen's house honing carpentry skills, building smaller vessels, while still listening to and learning from their elders. The property where they gathered had Quonset huts and small workshops and looked like a shanty town. Susannah had wandered through it on the day of the piano party while exploring, and it was still owned by the octogenarian and former shipyard owner, Otis John Gregory. It was now occupied by semi-squatters, men who eventually became known as the rusticators. The term *rusticator* is used primarily by Mainers to describe families who came to the state in the late 1800s and settled in camps and cabins for the hunting season. The word *rustic*, which relates to rural living, could even be the precursor to the term "living off the grid" which summed up Owen's way of life. *Rusticators* suited them all, however, and became the term in Ossonet to describe those who stayed on in the shipyard long after shipbuilding had come to an end.

The rusticators made their living doing piecemeal work in metalsmithing, engine repair, woodworking, and fine carpentry. They always kept their workshops around the yard and were the dwellers of the small sheds and shanties that Susannah had originally thought was an old logging camp. This small group of men believed that Owen Dodd was the most talented one among them, and the only one with the private property to be left alone to fulfill their destiny and revive shipbuilding on the site where it all began.

Apart from Owen and the rusticators, it felt as if the rest of the town and the whole state of Maine were changing, modernizing fast, and were clearly at risk of forgetting their glorious shipbuilding past as more realtors started sniffing around these quaint towns. It was Owen's first instinct when he saw Susannah in his yard, and realtors were scouring the state of late, looking for properties to put on the market. The people of Ossonet, for now, accepted the old shipyards as part of the scenery, but they were itching for change and the money that comes with it. Some were being encouraged to sell old family properties while other, more affluent newcomers to town, wanted a marina for their small fiberglass and aluminum boats. There were shell fishermen making a living off the clam flats nearby and former shipyards with rich history, but it was all up for grabs now.

Owen had been texting Susannah at the paper since the piano-burning party out of a sense of desperation. He and the rusticators sensed that they had to do something. Susannah seemed curious enough to be trusted. He wasn't sure but he was running out of options.

Just that morning, he had observed that the harbormaster and a marine surveyor were talking about putting a few pilings into the water off the Dodd property to test the currents around it. The sample pilings were directly in front of Owen's property. The surveyor was considering what an expansive marina might look like. If they developed the area, Owen would never again be able to launch a schooner from his shipyard. A schooner built in the shipyard needed a bilgeway to splash down into the water. If a marina were built and pilings were added, he could never launch a schooner in the traditional Ossonet way, and it would be too heavy and expensive to do it any other way.

Having a noisy marina in front of his yard, with the possibility of a waterside restaurant being built, also made him worry that the town would place restrictions on what he could build on his property. Like many who were settling in Maine today or buying second homes, they saw it as a recreational paradise. To Owen and the rusticators, recreation was a threat to their shipbuilding dreams. After the harbormaster had left, Owen had discreetly gone out to the pilings and with a chainsaw had cut them at the water's edge. When the harbormaster came back from lunch, it was high tide. He and the marine surveyor were scratching their heads trying to figure out where the pilings went. When they later found them floating downriver, they rightly suspected Owen of cutting them.

When Susannah arrived she found six men on their hands and knees crawling around the loft floor as if they were engaged in some kind of intensive group therapy session. As they moved around on the floor, hunched over, they were mumbling to each other, almost like speaking in tongues. Yet this was not an Evangelical church service, and Susannah had already determined it was not a cult. But this was odd. They were not carrying religious objects, but as they crawled along, they held long flat sticks and thick sharp pins with fat yellow screwdriver heads. They had notepads, extra red yarn, and yellow pins in hand. The loft floor was about sixty feet long and twenty feet wide, so they were covering a lot of ground. They pushed large pins into the loft's corkboard floor and lined them up next to the sticks, which were being laid out in a very organized pattern. They wrapped the red yarn around the pins and crawled farther along the floor.

"This will be the measurement from the keel to the deck, right Owen, just above this point?" Seb asked as he crawled along ahead of Owen.

They all looked at each other.

Seb finally stopped crawling and asked, "Right?"

"God damn if I know," Owen finally said. "I've never done this before!"

Whack! One of the rusticators had tossed the wobbly piece of wood ahead of him, almost like casting a fishing line, and it made a "lofting sound"' as Owen called it.

They kept at it, and between the sound of long, wobbly, flat-sided wooden battens hitting the floor and Owen calling out measurements for Seb and the others to write down, it sounded to Susannah like they were playing a game of dominoes and were keeping score.

Smack! Whack! A new piece of wood hit the floor. Then they called out a number.

"Six and a half feet at the curve," Owen said as he measured out the size and length on the floor. "Got the numbers, Seb?"

They crawled behind the wooden battens with pins and red yarn that they were wrapping. It began to look like they were playing a life-size game of cat's cradle. They then slapped down another batten or flat stick that extended another twelve feet in front of them. They then resumed crawling, placing pins along the cork-like loft floor.

Seb peered at the red string that ran along the floor. He pulled out a ruler to count the feet, marking it down at different intervals along the floor with his number two pencil. Each time he finished writing the number down, he put the pencil behind his ear and crawled farther along the floor to check the next measurement.

"Check the numbers while I start thinking," Seb told Owen, and held up a beer bottle that had been sitting at the end of his long crawl across the floor. Susannah wondered if they had decided to try a mock-up of a large vessel for something to do. Owen had told her that they were always tinkering around with things and ideas. But this was a bit different.

Owen stuck a final sharp pin into the corkboard floor and dragged some red string over to one of the rusticators. She could now see what they had done. Using string, pencils, and battens, they had lofted the entire length and measurements of a schooner. Its outline was made of the wood pieces, the yellow pins, and the red string, but it did look like a boat.

Seb stood up, dusted off his knees, and walked across the floor carrying his bottle of beer. He was wearing a porkpie hat and overalls. He tipped his hat to Susannah as he passed her. Owen had recently told her that Seb had lost his right eye in a childhood accident and compensated for his diminished vision when doing carpentry by leaning his head slightly to the side while he worked—putting all his focus on the work with his only good eye. Owen had also told her that because of the way he had to lean, Seb had nearly sliced his skull when working too close to a blade once, and for that reason he had always worn a hat of some kind. He was never without a hat, and they often had pins with slogans attached to them. While some people collected pins from their trips to national parks, Seb sent out messages with his pins. This one quoted Ben Franklin: "There cannot be good living where there is no good drinking." At the piano burning party, Susannah had noticed he was wearing a pin that said, "If I am not back in five minutes, just wait longer." Seb handed a cold beer to Owen and the others and they clinked their bottles together.

Susannah was still not certain what this story tip was for the paper, but after living and studying the fading traditions, dress, and way of life of a minority tribe somewhere in the Mekong river valley, watching them in the loft that day made her start to wonder if she had stumbled into some unfamiliar tribal ritual that both baffled and intrigued her.

Just then Owen said, "Look out, you're standing on the line I just drew. That is going to be the bow."

She opened her empty notebook, suddenly feeling very much on the spot.

"Close that now," Seb said, and gently gestured for her to put away the notebook. "This is a big story."

He cleared his throat and leaned back against a drafting desk. "We're going to staht splittin' a big log this weekend," Seb said. It didn't sound like a very promising headline, and she could picture the look on her editor Bill King's face if he read a headline that said, "Owen Dodd and Team Split a Log."

"Got anything else?" she asked him. Owen looked annoyed at that remark.

"Should I tell her?" Seb asked Owen. He nodded yes. "We got word the other day some company has an eye on the area around the Dodd property in connection to a new marina, condominiums, and a restaurant."

"Means I will never be able to launch a schooner from here again, if it goes through," Owen said. Susannah felt a sudden twinge of compassion for Owen, and while they paused to see what she might say next, she was distracted again by his green eyes. She was embarrassed to stare at him, but he was far more attractive than she initially thought. He seemed less gaunt and tight-lipped. His face was fuller, his hair was thicker. His eyes had the color of the coastal waters in springtime when all the plankton blooms. They sparkled a bit when he talked. To her, he no longer looked like a tall, thin reed with a serious demeanor but was instead more stout, strong, and broad in appearance. She thought he also looked great in his tan work pants and cap, and perhaps this lofting work was part of his changed appearance.

"When was the last time a schooner was launched here?" she ventured, trying not to reveal her attraction to Owen or seem too disinterested in what they were telling her. She was still convinced there was no actual story here today, just some guys hanging out in a barn loft 'lofting,' whatever that meant.

"It was 1947," all the men said at once. "The *Katarina M.*"

"Don't you know your town history by now?" Owen teased.

"Oh, yeah. That was the last time the Paul Revere church bell rang," she said confidently.

"Well, except for weddings, funerals, and every Sunday," Seb noted.

CHAPTER THREE

Susannah got a big no from her boss on her story idea. Even though she explained that she had witnessed the "lofting of a schooner" in a dusty old barn, her editor wasn't impressed. She explained it was the next step after carving a half-hull model.

"Meh," he said. But there was a freshly carved half-hull model now in the barn, in a place where a hundred models from the past were a testament to what happened there, she told him.

"They are going to start to split some logs this weekend too," she added. "For planks and stuff." "Is that a story?" replied her editor after yet another meeting. Fact was, to her editor, it sounded more like a woodworking class—and there were plenty of those going on up and down the coast of Maine.

Susannah felt drawn to Ossonet not only as a journalist but as an anthropologist. She saw a proud culture trying to preserve its dying traditions—and it was happening on her news beat! She wanted to report on it far more than she wanted to write about the new sewage treatment facility. She was using her ethnological skills, which she saw as the study of aspects of humans within past and present societies, or more to the point, the origin and development of human societies and culture. This shipbuilding culture was making its last stand just as the real estate agents were swarming. Maybe it was an amateur pursuit, and she could hear her ex, Eric Strand's, famous line: "Anthropology is a field that has a low bar for entry, and a high bar for proficiency." But she was inspired.

Unable to say no to her again, Bill King gave her some more time to get a story. He still assigned her to the sewage treatment beat and anything to do with the highway department. She dutifully drove around the county looking for street closings and parts of the county that were going to have their roads paved. She usually found herself instead heading to Ossonet. It lifted her spirits for the first time in a while as the breakup with Eric had left her heart-broken, especially because while he went on to gain a professorship at a British university, she ended up back home living with her parents. He had urged her to "find her passion." Easy for him to say after she did so much fieldwork for him, but she had found a journalism course at a community college, and the man teaching the class took a bit of pity on her after hearing her story. He showed her that the old ways of print journalism were a lot like fieldwork, as it was about news gathering and observation. It sounded like cultural anthropology. She liked that. He suggested that she work for a publication someplace where there were still cultural traditions and even different dialects. He told her that the best place for this, where there was a strong tradition of maintaining regional print newspapers and a spirit of community journalism, was in the state of Maine. She was beginning to believe she might keep her anthropological skills sharp enough so she could resume some kind of fieldwork as she had done with Eric. And she liked that when going to Ossonet and the Dodd property, she never quite knew what to expect.

She had already watched them split gigantic logs and run them through the sawmill. But the project had progressed some, and on this day, as she drove up the dirt road to the Dodd shipyard and adjacent house, Owen was in the middle of a field of freshly cut timber, holding a big black pencil and what looked like a curved ruler or batten. Surveying the crowded field of wood, he was wearing a top hat and looked a bit like a maestro directing his attention to every member of this cut timber orchestra all around him. He would gesture with his big pencil toward one piece, then, in a flourish, he would point his pencil at another one and in a change of tempo, he would leap to another piece, crouch down, and start to draw out a curved line with his arched ruler. As she watched, mesmerized by what he was doing, she forgot about the ensemble of wood cuts and tripped over a massive slab of timber and fell between two flat pieces, incurring a few scrapes and a splinter.

"Heh, look out for that," Owen said without looking up. "You okay? I am sketching the shape of a scantling."

"A what?" She nodded yes as she got up and readjusted herself.

"Scantling. When you cut the timber to build the frames for a schooner, they start off as scantlings."

"So, a log turns into a scantling turns into a frame?" she asked, pulling the splinter from her knee and trying to keep up on this process, but she was a bit lost. A scantling?

"From a scant thing to a futtock to frame a schooner—in the end." Owen was looking around for the large piece of wood he had already marked to bring over to the band saw. "Want to help?" he asked.

She had never hauled wood, except to stack pieces beside a fireplace. This was heavy and unwieldly, and she tried to hold on as Owen dragged it to the old shipyard band saw and lifted it onto a massive metal slab that was smooth and cold, with the huge, serrated blade running down the middle of it. They wrestled the wood onto the large flat slab of metal. She felt like this wood had just been placed on the operating table and was about to go under the knife.

"This thing really works?" she asked nervously. It had last been used to cut wood for framing a schooner in the 1940s. Owen and the rusticators had kept the machine going for other smaller projects. It was rudimentary in its technology but perfect for the task at hand. Owen grabbed some safety glasses for her. He wore none, but she thought better of it and put them on, making it harder to see through the smudged glasses.

"Starts hard but it's a workhorse. Brace yourself against the slab. See, like this." He walked behind her and wrapped his arms around her waist to show her how to stand. It was necessary, as he needed to demonstrate how she should lean in. But she had not expected him up this close. "Whatever you do, don't lean too far forward. Keep your head back." And he touched her hair and coaxed her head back. "The saw alone could slice your skull in half." He checked her stance and said, "Press your hips into the machine but keep your upper body leaning out. Got to stay clear of that blade. Better pull your hair back or wear this hat," Owen said, handing her his top hat.

She nervously tucked her hair under the hat, and with the goggles, she figured she looked the height of steampunk fashion. Fashionable or not, her skull and eyeballs were protected. Owen then went to the other side of the slab so they each had a grip on the timber with about six feet between them and the blade at the center. He pointed to a big red on-off switch above her head and said, "Are you ready? You're closest, so hit that switch. Go."

She nodded and hit the big red button. The machine rumbled to life, and the deadly blade whirred fast and sharp. Susannah shuddered and leaned back, but Owen immediately began pulling the thick oak plank against the whirring blade so as she held on to it, she was pulled forward, while leaning back, safely away from the middle.

Owen guided the wood along the blade, following the sketched, curved lines on the thick wood. The antique machine was equipped with a wooden lever with numbers one through twenty. Owen had marked his scantlings with numbers as well. He shouted over the noise of the machine, "Call out the number as we reach it!"

She tried to read the number and shout while still steadying the wood without pushing herself too close to the blade. She was tempted to throw off the hat and goggles as she could not see very well, but she was too afraid of the blade. Meanwhile, Owen continued to steer it and turn it according to the penciled-in numbers. The wood slab was hard to push through while also following the lines.

As they cut, she could see how the numbers on the band saw and written on the scantlings allowed them to make an accurate, nice curve in the wood. As the plank moved heavily through the saw, the curves emerged. Calling out the number seven, she turned the wood slightly; and then eight, another slight turn; then nine, and she shifted her weight to help push it up to ten. The wood tapered off at an angle, and when they reached twenty, it was through. They had cut something that resembled the shape of a harp. Owen dashed over to her side and reached over her to hit the off button.

Susannah jumped back from the machine. She bent over with relief and exhaustion, taking off the top hat and glasses.

"That was terrifying!" she exclaimed. She was amazed by how good it felt, however, to cut wood that way.

"Fun, huh?" Owen had to admit he was impressed with her work, and her sun-bleached hair.

"Better put the hat back on," he said.

They finished six more scantling cuts over the course of the morning and early afternoon. She completely forgot about her assignment but did let Bill know she was working on the shipyard story.

He had a few questions.

"My boss wants to know, how long is this whole thing going to take?" she asked. "And how are you going to pay for it?"

"Tell him it's hard sayin,' not knowin,'" Owen said.

"He won't like that answer," she said, but she didn't press the matter.

She helped him carry the scantlings into the barn. He explained that the large, cut curved pieces would be clamped and attached to another piece to become futtocks. Two futtocks screwed together made a piece of a frame. Once the frames were put together, this would be the first in many "double-sawn oak frames" that would be raised up on the keel and would eventually become the skeleton of a sixty-foot ship. "Ever seen an old photograph of the ribs of a whale?" Owen asked her. "It looks a bit like that before framing."

Susannah was still trying to recover from the reverberations of the band saw and was not taking notes. In the barn, out of the sun, she felt her sweat cool as she stood and watched the water from the river basin lap past. She noticed a gentle whirlpool in the basin as the tide ebbed and flowed around it. As he talked, she listened to the river now lapping under the barn. It was so close to the water's edge that small boats could be built inside it and launched right out the back of it. When the tide was very high, anyone in the barn would be stranded and must wait out the tide or paddle over to the house in a small boat. Owen pointed out the place where the town wanted to install more pilings. She felt a strong urge to step closer to him.

"Seriously, now, how are you going to afford to do all this?" she asked.

"Free labor helps." He patted her shoulder and smiled. "Got us some scantlings cut anyhow," he quipped.

Over the next week, she tried to focus more on her newspaper assignments. She learned more about the Clydebank harbor cleanup efforts while also driving around the county, checking on work projects and road closings. The latter would be considered one of the lowest level assignments for a journalist, but Susannah's mind was more happily distracted by the happenings in Ossonet. She told her boss she would update him later that day on any developing story. She was daydreaming as she drove along a westbound road toward her new favorite town and got stuck behind an old WWII-era flatbed truck. It was going about 15 mph in a 40 mph zone. From a couple of cars back, she could hear grinding gears and see the exhaust smoke. An arm was gesturing from the driver's side for all cars to pass, so she eventually did. She looked over at the driver of this contraption. It was Seb! The truck was loaded high with scrap metal, and she noticed a vintage baby crib, pewter pots, brass doorknobs, and what looked like a tuba, a trumpet, and some tarnished copper gutter pipes. Two of the rusticators were squatting in the back on the flatbed with rope—it seemed to keep things from falling off. They looked like the ragmen her grandmother used to talk about during the Great Depression.

She watched Seb gesturing with hand signals that they were turning right, which meant they were heading to the Dodd yard. She raced ahead and luckily had her camera ready to capture them as they came clinking and clanking down the old road toward the Dodd property. She thought the photo might be one more way to convince her editor she had a unique story here. They came down the hill and headed straight toward the barn. The truck seemed to be moving a bit too fast.

"Seb!" Owen yelled. "Use the clutch! And the hand brake!"

The truck was rolling toward the edge of the riverbank as Seb put it into low gear. Owen quickly tossed some wooden blocks in front of it to stop it moving, and then Seb gave it all he had and pulled hard on the emergency brake. It screeched and groaned with the effort, but one more tug and another wood block and it finally stopped rolling.

Susannah was taking photos of this scene when Owen said, rather sternly, "Can you please put away your camera?" He blocked her lens with his hand. Then he put up both hands, just as she was focusing her camera. "This is *not* for your story."

She was puzzled, even offended that he did not see she was a working journalist on the job. He had not been this cold before, either.

"I'll show you, but I am not going to tell you what is going on," he finally said. He and Seb and the rusticators started unloading the metal and carrying it to the far end of the property, out of view. There was a huge, growing pile. They all stood around silently, nervously looking at Owen, who also wasn't making eye contact with anyone. He finally said to the others, "We can melt it all down tonight and pour it into the mold after dark. We will have a keel then."

Susannah had been learning that the keel is considered the

backbone of a schooner, and for centuries the only metal that did the job right was lead. A keel could be made of mostly wood, but it must include some dense metal at its lowest point. She had hoped to include some interesting sidebars in her story like this but was now concerned Owen was being too secretive. Without lead, there is no way a vessel can stay upright and balanced. Because lead was always the de facto metal for a keel with its stabilizing weight and density, during World Wars I and II, many wooden ships were seized and scrapped to get to the lead. Many historic American schooners and wooden vessels met their demise when they were seized or given up for the war effort. Their lead keels and ballast bricks became lead bullets and tanks.

Susannah had not considered that lead was exorbitantly expensive and not exactly something Owen could afford. The men knew the Ossonet technique of making a lead keel, and all they really needed to do was melt all the scrap metal and pour it into a mold. Any lead spilling into the clam flats would destroy a livelihood and might bring every shell fisherman in the county to Owen's house to shoot him at close range. If anyone in town caught on to what they were doing, they would blow the whistle on them.

"There is a new moon," he said to Susannah, "so it's going to be darker than a pocket tonight. Say nothing to no one."

He assured her it would not spill. She worried if it did, she would have to write about it.

"I think it's probably best if you don't stick around today," he said, and she agreed. "I will give you an update about it."

Over the course of the long night, piece by piece the items containing lead were melted down in a huge cast iron drum over an open fire; and as it melted, Owen and the rusticators used a kind of bucket brigade to carefully haul the liquid metal and slowly and carefully pour it into the trough. They had built a thirty-foot wooden mold near the scrap pile, and it was lined with foil to keep the wood from cracking or even igniting into a chemical fire. As they poured the melted metal, a whiteish liquid flowed and splashed along like a silver river. As the trough filled, the lead started to settle and harden and soon looked like pearl-colored cream. It was almost tempting to touch, but of course, molten lead would boil a hand or arm right off.

Owen, Seb, and the others continued to melt and pour the lead well into the dark night, using flashlights and the light of the fire to see.

They spoke very little, and when they did, they barely whispered. They were all keeping an eye across the river basin for anyone official and prayed that they were elsewhere on patrol that night.

By morning, they were exhausted but had not left the site. However, the evidence of melting lead was hidden. It had cooled and gelled enough in the trough to no longer be a lethal liquid, but it was still not quite a solid form. It had to cool.

So, they sat, drinking hot black coffee around a small fire.

Owen stretched out his legs, got up, and very lightly tapped the lead just once to assure himself it was cool.

Later, he called Susannah at the newspaper office.

"I have a good story for you," he said. "We got a keel!"

In this case, Susannah gave the phone to Bill. She did not want to be complicit in their white lie. He took Owen's word for it and figured it was a big enough story to print. He gave it a headline based on what concocted story Owen told him:

Keel Arrives from Canada at Historic Ossonet Shipyard.

CHAPTER FOUR

One of his first visitors to the yard after the word got out that a large keel had "arrived from Canada" was Otis John "O.G." Gregory and his daughter, Janet. Now ninety-four years old, Otis Gregory had briefly been the scion of the nearby Gregory shipyard, and as a young man, he witnessed the final launch of the *Katrina M*. His family's business went into bankruptcy in the early 1960s, but the property was intact and eventually was populated by the rusticators with their shanties and workshops. While the town thought of it as an abandoned property and an eyesore, O.G. was a proud man and still dressed and carried himself around his derelict property like a shipyard owner. He dressed even more formally when going to another shipyard owner's property, so he arrived at Owen's wearing his best trousers and tweed jacket, a bowtie, and his porkpie hat. He waved an arthritic hand to Owen as his daughter helped him out of the car.

Owen brushed off the sawdust and came over to shake hands with the only other living shipyard owner in Ossonet.

"Got a keel, O.G.," Owen said, pointing at the lead beam now lying in the dirt. "How about that?"

O.G. nodded his head in approval. "Ayuh. Got to authenticate it before you do anything else," he said in a raspy voice, mentioning a shipyard superstition that shipbuilders must first 'authenticate the keel' to mark the beginning of the construction of a ship. It was sometimes referred to as 'laying' the keel.

"Got to make sure the keel is truly and fairly laid," he told Owen. The old expression made Owen and Janet giggle, but O.G. was right.

They needed a ceremony.

His forty-two-year-old daughter, Janet, had stood by patiently as her father and Owen talked. Although she was as familiar with the Dodd yard as anyone, having grown up with the family, she did not consider shipyards to be sacred places as her father and Owen did. She had recently returned from a decade of living in Colorado. She came home, a bit reluctantly, to figure out how to help her aged widowed father but hoped to soon return to the West. She wore her long dirty-brown hair pulled back in a single braid and refused to change out of her favorite cowboy boots. She often felt confined by the smaller spaces around New England and the boots made her feel Western. Even though Maine was a vast state with a lot of wildernesses, it was not the West. She was also not a typical Ossonet native in that she had seen something of the world. Yet she also had a native's insight into the town. She knew the Dodds almost as well as her own family, and she, too, could see big changes coming to the region. As a Gregory, she shared that Pilgrim's pride in that she also came from a distinguished line of flinty Maine shipbuilders whose ancestry dated back to the Mayflower. Also, she was delighted that her father could see this, even if her frail dad's poor mobility and eyesight meant that he could no longer see or hear as much. Coming to the Dodd yard was a highlight for him. He would go there every day if he could, but today he had an appointment to keep with his doctor.

"We have to get going, Dad," Janet said. "You've been talking about that piece of lead for about an hour now!"

"We're going to see a schooner in frame again," he declared excitedly to his daughter as she led him back to the car. "A schooner in frame!"

She could see his eyes welling up with emotion. It pleased her to see him so excited about something again.

As they pulled out of the driveway, O.G. rolled down the window and called, "Now do have a proper ceremony, young Owen. Do it before the frame goes up! Get that keel true and properly laid."

Janet and Owen gave each other that funny look but knew enough to take it seriously.

"Got to lay the keel," her dad insisted. "And do some speechifying."

The plan to authenticate the keel was set for the following week, and Susannah was asked to alert the *Clydebank News*. She expected it might be a small story, but Bill decided that he would send his senior reporter, Francis, and a photographer, too.

Since she was not on assignment, Susannah offered to help with what Owen called a "keel-laying" shindig. They were going to serve beer and hot dogs, and Owen had a few other surprises planned. Susannah met up with Owen's parents and siblings who had come to help, and they brought a cake and more hot dogs. Susannah helped set up. Owen's mother was being very gracious about the fact that Susannah was interested in the story, and she naturally wondered if maybe this young woman was interested in her son, since she had been coming to the yard a lot. Janet Gregory also came by and offered to help. She, too, had the impression that Susannah was Owen's sweetheart.

"So, how long have you been seeing Owen?" Janet asked casually after they had been standing together a while serving hot dogs to the growing crowd.

"Not." Susannah shrugged. She had not meant to sound cold. Instead, Susannah felt a wave of embarrassment.

"Oh," Janet smiled. "Give it time."

Owen had come up with the idea to have felt tip markers available so people could write something on the keel. There was not much to say about a piece of lead lying in the grass, although there was now thick oak built around the lead so the whole piece was about forty feet long. The keel would be the backbone of the entire vessel but seldom seen again. People wanted to leave their mark, much like construction workers expressing themselves on the girders before a new high-rise building is covered with concrete and glass. Everyone had something they wanted to write on the keel, as if each person were sending out their own message in a bottle. They covered the keel with quotes like "Don't Sink" or "Safe Voyage" or "Be Wary of Davey Jones Locker" or "Batten Down the Hatches!" Others just wanted to mention loved ones with: "To Jack, We Miss You" or "To Bill and Marion, my parents," while a teenager confessed her feelings when she wrote "I love Kevin B." Another mysterious person noted, "Schooner man. I still love you."

Owen's surprise was they had decided to bring the first frame out of the barn as part of the keel-laying ceremony, and they had spent much of the week building it. The huge frame was wide and thick in the middle, and then tapered toward the top. The curved frame must have been twelve feet high and fifteen feet wide and weighed at least a thousand pounds. It looked like the ceiling frame of many of the churches around New England, which were usually built by shipwrights. Flipped upside down, the frames of a schooner resemble to a tee what the sanctuary of an old New England church looks like, where massive beams come together in a perfect arch.

As the afternoon wore on and their hot dog and felt pen supply ran low, Susannah and Janet walked over to the barn to ask Owen when they would be ready. He told them to prepare to ring the bell.

The men rustled into position around the frame, while Susannah and Janet rushed back to the house, where Susannah rang the bell to get people's attention. She felt awkward about being so key to announcing something to people she hardly knew, and she was glad when Janet shouted, "The keel-laying ceremony will begin!"

Owen walked out of the barn. He looked confident and calm as he waited for people to quiet down. He wiped his brow and removed his cap. His hair was sticking straight up, but he flattened it back down with his hands. As Susannah was about to take a picture, she suddenly heard the click, click of a high-speed digital camera, the same whirring sound she'd heard at sporting events when the photographer takes rapid fire shots. The huge lens focused on Owen, as one of the photojournalists from the *Clydebank News* did his work. She felt a twinge of satisfaction that her friend, possibly her new man, was newsworthy.

When Owen got everyone's attention, he said in a somber voice, "This keel-laying marks the start of the construction of a schooner. This vessel's keel is well and truly laid. Its destiny begins." He then turned to the barn and yelled, "FRAME UP!"

Suddenly, fifteen men came out of the barn, carrying the heavy double-sawn frame over to the keel. Then, just like a barn raising, they heaved it up together to its full height, stretching their hands to the sky. The crowd gasped and then cheered.

Susannah could hear the camera clicking behind her and felt a sudden swell of emotion and excitement. People continued to clap. Some shouted "Huzzah! Huzzah!" She looked over toward an emotional O.G. and Janet. The whirring cameras focused on Owen and the rusticators. She took her own shot of O.G. as he leaned on his walker. For centuries, shipwrights had yelled *FRAME UP!* as they built thousands of schooners. Those two words had not been uttered in town for nearly seven decades, and O.G. had longed to hear them again throughout his long life. Susannah captured the emotion on his face as the past collided with the present for him. *FRAME UP!* was more than words for the old man.

To Owen's delight, he could look up and see the frame above his head. He could imagine it slowly emerging as a schooner "in frame," but this was just the beginning. His eyes met O.G.'s, and the two men nodded. O.G. tipped his cap to Owen while Owen, Seb, and the rusticators slowly walked back into the barn and out of sight. Once inside the barn, they could not contain their excitement. They slapped each other on the back, hugged, letting out their own cheers.

The crew came to the barn door as O.G. had managed to get to the barn with his walker and was extending his arthritic hands. Owen instead gave him a gentle hug.

"Got you something to celebrate, O.G.," Owen said, smiling.

O.G. put his hand on Owen's shoulder. "A schooner in frame again. If it couldn't be a Gregory to do it, I am glad it was a Dodd."

"We'll get it done, ayuh!" Owen said.

"You will, son, you will," and then he laid down the gauntlet. "No Gregory shipwright ever took more than three seasons to build and launch a schooner. Got to get this thing done by next spring." As he maneuvered away to join his daughter, the old man mumbled to Janet, "They're going to need some more men to help them along or they'll never get it done."

During the celebration, Susannah had watched her colleague Francis making notes as he covered the event, doing the job that she should have been doing. She asked him, "I was surprised our editor gave you this assignment?"

Francis said, "Yep. Bill told me to get over here last minute. Should be great!"

"But I have the backstory and all the notes and have spent a lot of time here," she complained, feeling a bit puzzled.

"Oh, I think he wanted the story to be objective, not personal. You are dating Owen, right?"

Susannah shook her head no.

"You're not?" he asked. "We both assumed you were."

"I kind of uncovered this whole story," she said, but realized she may have gotten too close to the source.

During the shindig, she got to know Janet better and even chatted awhile with Owen's parents. Perhaps she was dating him but didn't know it? She had come to the town out of curiosity and was intrigued by a man she felt was its most beloved native son. She had not thought it through, however, as she was increasingly spending all her free time in his world. He really didn't seem that interested in hers. In fact, long after the frame was raised, he and the rusticators had been sitting and talking, rehashing the day, smoking cigarettes, and drinking all the beer in their barn fridge. They had an extra stash cooling in the creek when they wanted more. There was no doubt it had been a great day for them, and the party was going to go late.

She decided it was time to go home and found Owen to say goodnight.

"Want to go downriver tomorrow?" he asked her. "For research purposes? I want to show you something."

Susannah tried to hide how pleased she was.

"What time?"

"Come over when the tide is turning," he said.

CHAPTER FIVE

Owen's hair was combed, and he was wearing a clean, albeit wrinkled shirt when she got to the rickety dock off Owen's property where he was waiting. The rusticators must have considered it a romantic date since he was wearing what they called his "going ashore" clothes. It seemed to cause a bit of a stir or some concern, perhaps, because as she walked through the Gregory yard, she bumped into Seb. He tipped his hat to her and then said something odd. "Going downriver?" he asked. "Got a date?"

"Just going downriver." Susannah rushed along to Owen's property. She had spent an hour trying to Google the tide charts for Ossonet as she had no idea when the tide turned.

"Nothing rarer than a rare day in June," Seb said. "Don't let Owen burn holes in you."

"Beautiful day," she nodded. She had no idea what he was talking about.

She reached Owen near the small skiff. As she looked around the river basin, she noticed a small mooring field of boats was bobbing empty, the boats chafing at their lines as if they too wanted to go out and play downriver. "You have a bathing suit, right?" he asked. She did, in fact, although the water in Maine was very cold.

"You will get wet," he added.

"As long as you don't burn holes in me," she said.

"Huh?" The motor had started, and he had not heard her. "Oh, Seb. He always says that about me. He thinks I am wicked intense sometimes.

33

"I think nowadays they call it hyper-focused," she replied.

"Huh?" He wasn't really listening.

She said loudly, "Hard of hearing?"

Owen revved up the engine and shrugged off her question. The small metal boat—the kind favored by shell fishermen who used this type of boat out on the clam flats—was very stable. Owen had one hand at the wheel, sitting on his haunches with his head tilted to one side. He looked around the river basin and occasionally pointed to something as if to show her his world a bit. Seeing him relaxed and looking a bit sportier out of his work clothes, she had begun to appreciate his singular style. She liked the way he kept a light hand on the wheel and knew every curve of the river. She realized that he had probably sat in this exact position, heading downriver every summer day for most of his life. It dawned on her she was probably not the first woman to go downriver with Owen Dodd. The twenty-two horsepower engine cut nicely through the flat water, out past the far shore, and beyond the railroad bridge which veered inland. The skiff turned offshore toward the larger bay and islands in the distance. She sat up front as he headed out to the open water. The boat settled into a rhythm on the slightly choppy wide open bay. Half serious and half amused, she decided if they went much farther out to sea and he tried anything rough, she'd make sure the oar lying in the boat was within reach—either to paddle back or to hit him with. Finally, Owen tapped her on the shoulder, pointing around the point of land they had passed. It was a pine-laden island with a big barren meadow at the top of a hill. He gestured that was where they were headed.

There was no beach for them to land the boat. Instead, they would need to climb out onto the marsh and haul the boat up on land a bit.

As they pulled closer to a high bank of mud and grass, Owen said, "Okay, we wade to shore from here, and I'll haul the boat out once we get to the land."

Susannah was trying to be helpful. She said, "Now?" and simply jumped into the waves and started wading through waist-deep water. Owen was still in the boat, taking off his shirt and long pants to keep them dry. He laughed and said, "I didn't think you would just jump in with all your clothes on!" The water was frigid, but they worked together to get the boat ashore. They could see their skin and clothes through the translucent, cold water.

Once they hauled the boat onto the shore, he said, "If you have any more dry clothes, you should change now. No one's around. Just me."

"Well, don't look," she said.

"Oh, look out for ticks. This island is covered with them," he added. "Check everywhere."

She shook off her wet clothes and quickly put on dry ones, checking her skin for the nasty bugs.

As they walked up the rather steep hill, side by side, she was swinging her arms and her hand tangled up with his by mistake. He didn't pull it away but instead held it. They climbed the hill holding hands, and at the top he pointed toward the vast ocean in the distance.

"From this hill, you can clearly see the spherical shape of the earth. See the horizon? It's curved."

He was right, there was no straight-edged horizon; it was clearly rounded like an orb. It was unusual to see the curve of the earth so clearly, and it was in part because they were on a small barrier island, up high, with not much between it and the North Atlantic. She leaned back to be closer to him as he put his arm around her waist. She started to wonder if this was where Owen took all his dates. He then casually dug a hand in his pocket and pulled out a coin and flipped it.

"Do you bring all the women you meet here to show them this?" she asked, feeling relaxed and flirtatious.

"Not yet," he said with a hint of sarcasm. "But anyone who comes here leaves knowin' that without a doubt, the earth is round. Can't you feel the gravitational pull?" He was charming. And he pulled on both her arms, so their bodies were now drawn together. "Seems you won the coin toss."

"What did you flip a coin for?" she asked.

"I flipped a coin after that first day I met you," he said. "I decided then that I would hopefully get you here. Now that you are here, I am just flipping it for you to witness."

She was thinking he meant "that I got you to this island" not "I got you to like me." He meant both.

"How about you flip it again? Two out of three," she teased.

"Well, you got in the boat with me, and you keep coming around," he insisted. "I will flip it again but heads or tails I am going to try to kiss you now." They didn't wait to flip the coin. His kiss was surprisingly gentle, and she held on longer for more.

"With the tide coming, we have time to walk down to the dunes over there." He pointed to a distant beach and a sweep of sand dunes. "We just have to get back here before the tide turns or we'll have a slower time getting back with the current."

They held hands as they walked down the hill, reached the water, and walked along the sand and beach grass. He led her to the path toward the higher dunes, past some wild cranberry bogs. He showed her deer tracks and said how the deer usually eat all the cranberries, but locals still come out in fall and harvest what's left for homemade cranberry sauce.

The cranberry bogs seemed to be in a protected area as there was a sign to keep out. "Are we allowed to be here?" she asked.

"Not really."

And they kept walking along a small trail while holding hands. Like most Mainers, Owen really didn't see any need to ask permission when it came to roaming on the protected islands, woods, and trails where he grew up.

"Let's duck in here," he said. There was a kind of sandy grove shaded by a few beach plum and eastern red cedar trees. "We can sit here awhile."

She sat in the shade of the sparse-looking cedar tree, out of the wind, as they were surrounded by the soft dunes. He placed a large, clean blanket that he had brought with him from the skiff onto the sand. Clever man that he was, she thought, he was planning on lying down here with her. As he wrapped his arm around her waist and she let his other hand lightly touch her breasts, they could embrace and kiss and feel the sand's warmth but not be covered or irritated by it. Touching her auburn hair or looking at her hazel eyes or her shapely breasts made him feel as if a long spell of bad luck were receding with the tide and something good was coming. He felt aroused by her, as she seemed as at home lying in the dunes as he was.

Meanwhile, her mind was working a little too much, and she wanted to talk to him more. "Do you ever come out here for like a bonfire?" she asked, feeling his caress as she now lay on her back, and he began taking off his shorts and shoes. They lay together for a while, listening to the sound of the ocean and seabirds, and touching fine, smooth white sand as he pulled her closer.

"Ayuh. Everyone comes downriver for that," Owen said, and then he touched her face and looked at her in a way that made her believe he wanted her in the same way she believed he was someone she could trust. "No laws here against boiling up some clams or lobsters for suppah."

"That sounds like fun. And. . ." She started to think of some more questions, but he interrupted her.

"Not sure how to say this without just sayin' it, but I want to fuck you so badly right now, I can think of nothing else."

"If we do, we will be done with just holding hands," she advised, worried about moving too quickly. "But, I have run out of questions and yeah, well. . . I have been thinking about it for a while now."

He kissed her hard then, and she could taste the saltwater on his lips against hers. He was lovely to look at, and she got a closer look at the rare color and pigmentation of those emerald eyes. She encouraged him then and could feel the tendons of his strong legs and arms pressing down on her. All that physical work made her feel like he could bear her weight and she took off her shirt and pulled herself up closer to his chest with her bare breasts. With one arm he rubbed her breasts and pulled down her pants while kicking off his shoes and clothes and getting a grip with his toes in the sand as he entered her.

CHAPTER SIX

Francis Hoyt's large feature story appeared on the front page of the *Clydebank News* two days after Owen and Susannah had been together "downriver." It was the kind of story Susannah could have and should have written as it had all the colorful details of the keel-laying ceremony and interviews with Owen and some of the rusticators. The family was mentioned, and Hoyt even had a chat with Mr. Otis Gregory. Everyone around Clydebank applauded Francis as it had been almost seventy-five years—give or take a month or two—since a story had been written about a schooner in an Ossonet shipyard. The story included photos of the men pushing the frame up, the community signing the keel, and Owen smiling and "speechifying" while most of the county residents were featured in the background.

The same day, Susannah was grappling with an uncomfortable amount of sand in her below regions after messing around in the dunes with the story's protagonist.

She got out of the tub and went to pick up the paper, which was delivered to her door. After reading Francis's cover story, she found herself feeling a bit ashamed, sitting in her apartment trying to soothe her private parts. It was the kind of local story that Susannah had been encouraged to write when she'd attended that newspaper conference right before she met Owen Dodd. As a journalist, she had uncovered a story unique to Maine, one that even a cultural anthropologist might find fascinating. She was pleased that her news gathering and curiosity brought the story to her editor's attention, but he had assumed she wasn't quite serious enough to handle the big story. They dismissed her as having a "crush" on Owen. She also knew she had now crossed a line, the same one she crossed with Eric, in that she was getting involved with the man and the work, and worried it would start to blur. Having lived and studied the fading traditions, dress, and way of life of a minority tribe for six months with Eric, she had learned and used her own instincts to immerse herself in a culture and a people whose way of life was quickly disappearing. In southeast Asia, as much as she became very attached to the people, particularly the women and children, she learned she must always remain an observer, and never, ever feign to become a part of the tribe. With her writing ability and instinctive people skills, she helped her professor boyfriend with the work of documenting his research.

Francis and Bill came to her desk as soon as she got in. She thought they were going to somehow thank her for leading them to this story. Arms crossed, with his bifocals on the tip of his nose, Bill said, "Well? When should I assign Francis to go back? What's next?" And Francis added, "Could I get an interview with Owen about next steps? Can you give me his cell number so I can set it up?"

They were thinking of making it an ongoing series, and Francis, as the senior reporter, would take the lead on it. Somehow, she would be in a secretarial capacity and set up meetings between Francis and Owen.

She was not only upset that she had been screwed out of a great story, but she had let herself down as a field researcher in anthropology. She knew better, that if even an amateur anthropologist wants to be accepted in an ancient culture, she doesn't get involved with the tribal chief. She had done exactly that.

She should have fought harder for what really was her story. It should have been assigned to her.

"If you want any updates on the project, you should check my blog or social media," she later said to Francis.

She had no blog but felt it was the only way to lay some claim to this story and maybe to Owen himself.

"OK, fine with me," Francis said. "But any journalist worth his salt should not be blogging. Blogs are not a reliable news source."

Susannah replied, feeling her face get hot and flushed with both embarrassment and annoyance, "In this case, I am very close to the source."

Maybe the blog idea wasn't so bad after all. She decided, after sending her missive to Francis, that she would ask Owen. She was going to be at his house that evening for more research, she told herself.

In fact, as summer went on, "getting to his house "or "going downriver" or "doing more research" was all she seemed to really think about and eventually write about. She named her blog *Downriver with Dodd* but did manage to keep the personal parts out of it. All summer long, whether it was in the living room, bedroom, or on the sand, the clothes came off the minute they were alone with each other. If she walked in the door in the evening, they lay down a blanket on the porch or on the living room floor. On weekends, they would float downriver and end up with their beach blanket in the dunes again.

In writing the blog, she kept the focus on the ship and slowly regained her story from Francis. As it was summer—the slow news months—most small city newspapers focus on the Fourth of July, parades, picnics, or outdoor activities, like fishing tournaments, baseball, and gardening. The news beats were easier, journalists could goof off a bit, so she wrote more about Owen on her own.

At first, the blog had a small following among a few locals who knew Owen.

Once there were a few more frames on the schooner, there was more to take photos of and read about. She put more of her energy into making the stories amusing, informative or fresh, and the readership grew. Meanwhile, Susannah's newspaper was at risk of becoming a handy firestarter. As the evenings got a little cooler, even though it was still August, she would walk in the door, hand him that day's paper, and while she was changing into comfortable clothes, Owen would usually flip through it and then open the woodstove door to start a fire.

"Wow, you read fast," she said, knowing he had only glanced to see if there were any stories about him in it.

"I'm sorry," he said. He sheepishly lit the newspaper on fire and all her daily work did give off a lovely, soft glow. He had already laid a blanket down in front of the woodstove.

"Can I make it up to you?" he suggested. "You can tell me what happened today in Clydebank."

She and Owen got down on the floor, taking off their clothes quite quickly.

"Let's add a little more newspaper," he suggested.

"Okay," she agreed. "Just not my stories!"

The woodstove fire intensified as he moved on top of her, pressing himself on her chest and belly and holding her arms slightly over her head. The fire was a bit too hot, and the night still humid.

"I got to open a window," she said. Owen released her as Susannah jumped up.

"Wait!" he called out. "Don't stand there naked like that!"

She quickly pulled the curtains shut and crouched down.

"The rusticators are probably watching," he warned.

The sheds of the Gregory shipyard were directly across the creek, and per usual the men were there. That night, they were also having a fire, burning wood scraps in a cast iron barrel, sitting on logs, and having a beer and a smoke in full view of the Dodd living room.

"Did you notice how they tend to sit on those logs, all facing our house?" Owen said. All Susannah heard was *our house*.

"I hope we're not putting on a nightly show for them." Susannah lay flat on the floor.

"Seb's probably cracking a beer and lowering his ass into his favorite viewing spot as we speak." Owen guffawed. "Must be a few rusticators over there now."

"I honestly hope they are not expecting a show." She trusted they were not voyeuristic. "Seems they prefer the bachelor life."

"Well, I wasn't the only one who noticed you at the piano-burning party, but I just happened to see you first," Owen said as he pulled her closer and wrapped his leg around hers, and then rubbed her breasts with his coarse hands. "I hope they did not see your breasts. I hope no one else ever gets to enjoy them like I am now."

"How is it that they didn't all fight over me?" she asked, stroking his hair and kissing him.

"Oh, they did a bit. They saw me flip a coin that night, and I think they got the message, but you have probably figured this out by now. There is only one Owen Dodd."

"Yes, I agree I could never handle two men like you," she noted.

"Heh!" he said. "Hope not."

He kissed her hard and began to run his hands down her belly toward the tufts of hair once covered by her panties. He was pulling those down now, slowly, and she was already wet with anticipation.

But her mind wandered to how they all deferred to him in a way that made him something of a feudal king, as he had the land and the birthright, and the rusticators didn't as such. His hand pressed down on her vagina and found the spot that caused her to stop ruminating and start moving with his body.

He stroked and poked and pressed her until she had forgotten the day and was just wanting him inside her when he whispered, "I was wondering, too, if your newspaper might do a story about how I need skilled shipwrights to work for free. Or maybe in the blog."

"Work for free? Are you sure?" She was breathing heavily now.

He had gone from fingers to mouth on her, and as he got hard and she stroked him he could not quite finish sentences, but he moaned, "Need to get more frames up by Christmas."

"Why Christmas?" she asked. And as he moved on top of her, she felt these pleasant, calming thoughts and feelings of being in love during the holidays.

"Got to frame her by Christmas," he explained. "Because after Christmas we have to get the planks on her by spring." They began to make love and she mumbled "Why spring?"

Grasping his back, she extended her hips and thrust herself upward as he penetrated her. It was intimate and felt good despite being on the hard floor. Soon, she could feel he was reaching orgasm. She quickly pushed her own hand down and rubbed herself to try and come when he did.

Suddenly, she thought she heard laughter. She gasped, thinking it was right outside the window. She wondered if the rusticators had pulled their chairs up closer as they heard their moans and whispering. During their lovemaking she had lost awareness of their proximity and didn't realize that their voices tended to carry across the creek on quiet nights.

"A wooden vessel," Owen said, just minutes after he had reached orgasm, "especially a newly built one, should never spend a summer on the hard. It needs to be in water." He pulled the blanket over them not realizing she was still pleasuring herself in order to climax. He was now looking towards the window. From his vantage point on the floor, he waved his hand toward the vessel outside the window. "It'll rot in place if the rain and sun beat down on her through another full summer."

He explained that it took too much time to build a massive shed for a schooner, and in Ossonet, schooners had always been built outside through all kinds of weather.

"The tradition is we build all our vessels outside, no matter what. We're like the post office. Come rain or snow or shine, we get it done in three seasons," he said. She had given up on having an orgasm and was lying still.

"No wonder shipbuilding didn't last here," Susannah joked.

As she said it, she thought she heard, very faintly, someone say, "Ayuh."

"Are the rusticators listening to us, Owen?" she said, pointing toward the creek.

"Probably," he laughed and started to get dressed. She enjoyed watching him put his clothes back on as they were taken off so quickly it was like he could simply step back into them in one motion. "Finest kind!" he said loudly as he tucked in his shirt. He wondered if they would like the compliment. "They're used to being a part of the conversation, I guess."

They were happy and tired after their evening together. They could see from peering out their window that the rusticators were congregated in the shed, drinking, talking, and maybe listening, but there was also a sole figure farther across the way, near the town landing, watching the house. Owen said, "That looks like a cop or a real estate developer. Either way, we don't want them hanging around near here. The less they hear or know, the better."

"Do you think the person way across the creek could hear us?" she asked.

He gestured to the window. "It's the guys over at the town landing, those realtor types and Weasel Martin's people, who would rather see us all gone. Got to get some young, skilled master shipwrights to come here soon or we will never launch by spring. They will have an official vote on this goddamn marina project at the next Town Meeting."

"What did they do in the old days when they needed men to work in the shipyards?" she asked.

Owen said, "They paid them."

"Do you think you could get them to come for any other reason?" she asked, wondering if they might also get inspired by the history here and the resurrection of shipbuilding in the town.

"Maybe. If I could find a few shipwrights who wanted to learn double-sawn frame shipbuilding, the real way it was done, they might find it worth their while. I have no idea how to find guys like that."

"Well, maybe the blog is not the best news source, but it sure can make this place look appealing, better than it actually is." She kissed him. Owen was quiet, but clearly someone thought it was a good idea as again she heard a faint "Ayuh." Then they both heard a rustling noise and although the tide was turning, and a puff of wind had come off the river just then, Owen was suddenly all business and got dressed. He said, "Be right back, beautiful. Don't go to bed yet. Got to talk to Seb a minute."

He stayed out late, so she finally went to bed. The next morning, Owen was asleep, so she spent a luxurious hour or more drinking coffee on the porch. She enjoyed watching the ripples of water as the tidal river ebbed and then flowed again past the barn and under the bridge. As the tide came or went, the opposing currents seemed to intersect not far from the barn, creating a whirlpool. The whirlpool was stronger than it looked, and it caught lots of flotsam and jetsam, sometimes taking a small log down in the whirl, only to find the log spit out again on the other side of the bridge. She had not seen stormy weather much that summer, but Owen said in a storm, the whirlpool grew in its power and was dangerous to anyone in a small boat when the tide was turning.

She had a journal on her lap and had begun writing that "things feel right on course." She paused after writing this and wondered if it might be bad luck to write something so affirmative. She had learned how a course change can be spotted by watching the wind or how calm currents in a changing tide might first ebb and then shift direction as the tide switched from "coming" to "going" and suddenly became more turbulent water to navigate through. She did not want turbulence. True, she was out of her depth with Owen in his profession as a master shipwright, just as she had been with Eric in his, but she felt strongly that Owen was attentive and loving and she did not want to mess with it now. She did love that the project was going slowly and the urgency to get it done was a bit lost on her. They had been living through a glorious Ossonet summer—a coastal Maine paradise where everyone heads downriver together in small skiffs in the early evenings after work and to the beaches and islands on weekends. On many occasions, she and Owen would pass by one of his lobster traps, and he would haul it up and always find a couple of lobsters. If Owen had a half bushel of clams that he got from a shell fisherman and some fresh corn from a nearby farm, they would invite Seb or Janet Gregory along. Other boats came too. They always found a spot in the dunes where they could have some shelter and a fire. They would add seaweed and beer to water, the New England way, and have a bona fide clambake. Heading downriver in a kind of flotilla of boats reminded Susannah of the musical *Carousel*. On the way home she would hum the 1958 lyrics she knew from the Rodgers and Hammerstein song, "A Real Nice Clambake."

Owen often rolled his eyes at this corny song, but Janet Gregory said that *Carousel*, which was filmed quite close by in Maine during the early 1960s, was her parents' favorite movie.

Susannah had also begun to feel very protective of her new relationship with Owen and the home where she was spending almost every evening and weekends. She didn't want to give up their sunny spot on the porch or their time on the river. She was happy in the old house with its intact fireplace from colonial times and box-like rooms with thick windowpanes that overlooked the water. She loved the old wooden floorboards and original beams. She was learning and gaining so much knowledge about this old culture. The place had grabbed her full attention, and she was gaining momentum with her blog simply by documenting Owen and his devotion to reviving an ancient craft. What the readers saw was intriguing just as Owen was to her.

When Owen came out on the porch and sat next to her, he kissed her and started rubbing her feet. He then reached over and stroked her hair.

"When you finish your coffee, I need you to come talk to the rusticators with me, okay?" he said out of the blue.

"The rusticators? Now?" She did not see any reason why she had to walk over to their side of the creek and talk to them on her nice day off.

But she reluctantly made the short walk down the road with him and across the creek bridge to where the rusticators had their shops.

There were usually about ten to fifteen rusticators in the yard at one time on a Saturday, where they did a lot of their contract work on projects then or just got caught up with each other.

It was early in the day, but they found Seb and six or seven other rusticators, including the very solitary Sam Dixey, who had known Owen all his life, standing around.

They entered a shed, and Seb motioned to Susannah that she should sit in an old rocking chair, which was the only piece of furniture in the shed. She sat down and realized straight off that the seat had an unobstructed view of the Dodd house across the creek. It was the first time she had ever looked over at what she had begun to think of as "their" home from this side of the creek.

From this vantage point, a rusticator would have a perfect view of the front room window where she stood naked the night before as she had pulled the curtains shut. Susannah noticed uneasily that there were also a lot of beer bottles and ashtrays scattered around the shed, but most of the chairs were turned inward, towards the stove. Fortunately, there was no sign of popcorn or front row seating facing the creek. She was relieved that she was not likely part of their nightly viewing.

Owen leaned against a workbench and fidgeted. Seb was wearing his work overalls and his signature porkpie hat. He had a salt and pepper beard stubble, but his hair still had a ruddy ginger color beneath the gray.

Susannah was beginning to fidget when he finally spoke.

"We are hoping you might agree with us when we say it is time for Owen to hurry up and finish his schooner."

She really didn't know what to say.

"Change is comin'," Seb went on. "We got word the other day the town may want to buy this property from the Gregorys. And a developer talked to Owen's father the other day. He told us some company has an eye on building that marina in front of the Dodd property. If they build a marina, the schooner will have no sea room to launch into the basin. The only way is to get her done over the winter and launch her in spring before the Town Meeting in June. We need help, we need more skilled hands."

"I am an old bum with one good eye." He smiled as he leaned in to look at her with his glass eye. "Most of us guys here are in our fifties and sixties, and what we need is younger, skilled guys who want to do this work for the experience as none of us have any money."

Susannah wondered why Owen hadn't told her all this, but she then realized that they had spent a lot of the summer goofing off, losing track of time, and maybe Seb decided to act.

She knew enough about local government that the town would have to vote. Properties could sell anytime but nothing could be built until after a town-wide vote.

"Ayuh," Seb was talking to the others. "Got to figure out a way for them to change their minds and vote against a marina."

"Or else the development and maybe sale of this place goes through?" she ventured.

"Ayuh," Seb said, and Owen looked down, his shoulders slumped.

"Got to find 'em soon," Seb noted. "We don't want just anyone, though. Got to be good."

She understood now why things had moved so slowly. Owen needed the manpower. The rusticators could not be counted on to do all the unpaid hard labor, nor should they.

"Whatever you can do, just so long as the town believes we are in the middle of something, not just the beginning," Owen said. "We want them to think this is well underway."

When she and Owen got back to the house, she asked, "If you got more men to work here, would they stay here?" Owen shrugged. He didn't know. She wondered if she should move in and at least claim her spot.

CHAPTER SEVEN

The leaves were starting to change color now and the woodstove was going almost every night, but the search for volunteer shipwrights was stalled. Owen wanted seasoned men, skilled workers willing to work outside all winter who wanted the experience of building a ship using the traditional Ossonet techniques. Susannah did her best with many blog posts and sharing photos about the glamour of working on such a unique, historic project. Her posts attracted many well-meaning people and earnest enthusiasts, but they had to first pass muster with Owen and the rusticators. Many came from newly developed suburban communities closer to Portland. They had the super-sized pickup trucks, freshly pressed Carhartts, crisp flannel shirts, shiny steel-toed work boots and new toolkits. They were mainly college-educated, newer arrivals to Maine and had brought all the cool stuff to do something rustic. But they had never worked in the trades. In fact, they often called someone to mow their lawns or fix a toilet.

The well-meaning volunteers would be offered a kind of obstacle course as a test to see how they did. One by one, Owen and the rusticators ran them through their paces and then proceeded to scare them off. Just as he had done with Susannah, he had them help him cut futtocks at the band saw. Over the roar of the machine, he shouted for them to call out numbers, warning them to steer clear of the blade. The whole time he barked at them, rattling each one. If they survived the band saw, he would jump over the scantlings like a mad wizard, telling them to pick the proper pieces for the next frame. When they picked the wrong one, Owen bellowed, waving his yardstick, "Full of knots!

No!" but gave them no further direction. When they tried to pick another one, Owen snarled, "Too many checks in the wood. No checks!" leaving them to try to figure out what Owen did want. He encouraged them to not use safety gear and to carry timber ten times heavier than the recommended weight. Owen exhausted himself trying to get rid of them, but if any of them persisted, he would then send them over to Seb and the rusticators to finish them off.

If the potential volunteers got as far as meeting Seb, Sam, and the others, they got quite a show. Inevitably Seb would put the fear of God in them. "Goddamn splinters," Seb would say as he dug his thumb into his eye socket, having hidden the fact that he'd removed his glass eye. "Doncha hate when you get something in yer eye?" He'd dig around, trying to remove a splinter.

"Ya know," Sam Dixey would explain, "it's really all fun and games here until someone loses an eye." And he'd point at Seb, who said, on cue as he popped his glass eye back in, "And then it's still all fun and games!"

Owen played the complete eccentric, as he would get a glint in his green eyes like he was slightly mad, but Seb took it to the next level.

The volunteer idea was not a bad one, but the men turned away just about everyone, leaving Owen working alone most of the time, and as November was fast approaching, what remained of the leaves on the trees around Ossonet had now changed to deeper autumn colors of gold and red.

It was late afternoon on a Friday and Owen was once again alone, working on putting together frame fourteen, when he heard a motorcycle pull into the shipyard. A man got off his bike and took off his helmet. His thick, wavy black hair was so voluminous it fell in front of his face. Owen noticed he was wearing a beaded leather coat. His coat looked handmade with both beauty and durability for working outside. He wore a small stone carving made of serpentine around his neck. It was unusual to see a man wearing such a beautiful piece of adornment.

He was also holding something in the other hand. Called a betel, it was central to double-sawn frame shipbuilding. The mallet was built with the most durable hardwood used to drive wooden nails into wooden planks and futtocks. Aside from an antique one Owen had in the shed, it was the first betel Owen had seen in years. He commented,

"Nice handle on that betel."

"Thanks," the stranger answered.

His name was William "Kip" Poucette. He told Owen he had read about the keel-laying ceremony and wanted to check out the old Dodd shipyard on his way back home.

"So, I heard something about you building a double-sawn framed schooner," Kip said. "Can I have a look?"

Owen felt that this might be the guy he was waiting for. "Let's go over to the band saw. Go ahead and pick a piece."

Kip deftly picked the correct pieces and carried them easily to the band saw. Together, they carefully cut a few scantlings as Kip called out the numbers. Then they carried the cut pieces together to the barn. Without fanfare, Kip used his betel mallet and hammered the scantlings with the wooden tree nails, or trunnels, creating the futtocks to piece together into a frame. With his wide shoulders and a strong grip, the trunnels went in easily.

Intrigued, Owen suggested they walk over the creek bridge to meet the rusticators. Kip stopped to grab a sack of something out of the saddlebag on his motorcycle. He also grabbed a hat, as the October day had started to grow cold. The hat was a thickly knit red stocking cap like those worn by the French voyageurs in the eighteenth century. It was a style popularized by French Canadian fur trappers; with his hat and broad shoulders, he looked like Fabian Fournier, the French-Canadian timberman from the Civil War era who was the inspiration for the Paul Bunyan myth.

They walked to the other side of the creek and found the rusticators standing around a cast iron fire pit burning scrap wood. At this time of year, the rusticators liked to be outside for as long as they could, keeping the fire stoked to stay warm. It was nearing dinnertime but none of them ever ate much, and they were settled in, already sipping beers.

To their surprise, Kip had a string of two freshly killed wildfowl in his sack.

"I thought you might like to cook these up," said Kip as he offered them by the necks. "Thought you might like roast duck for dinner?"

"What's the matter, have you all gone vegetarian?" Owen kidded the rusticators. Owen knew the rusticators did not really have any skills in that way. He wondered what Kip was up to.

They gingerly passed the ducks from one to another, but none of them really knew what to do with them.

Kip felt reassured that these guys were simply shipwrights and probably didn't care much for hunting or guns—and that was fine with him. They were all far more interested in the tool Kip was carrying. Any wooden shipwright worth his salt knew it to be called a "betel" but had no idea where the name came from. It was strongly believed that a wooden mallet was far smarter than banging a metal sledgehammer into the side of a wooden ship. As Kip stood talking to the men, he rested the betel on his boot. The rusticators' eyes kept wandering to the beautiful betel handle with its intricate inlaid woodwork. They admired its joinery and shape. It had obviously been handmade by a talented woodworker. Seb handed him a cold beer and decided not to give him the old glass eye routine. What they didn't know was he had been standing around having a beer with fellow shipwrights most of his life. Kip cracked the bottle open with his rigging knife.

The "interview" eventually became just a conversation when Kip finally told them that he was finishing a job at Richardsons Boat Yard on Great Morse Island where Kip grew up and lived part of the year. The other part of the year he lived in New York City. Kip thanked them for taking the time to talk, and before he left, he said, "I could put in a call to Neville Joseph, too. He might be interested in what you all are doing. I will get back to you, Owen."

Owen did not hear from him for over one week, but he knew Kip was his best shot at getting the boat done by spring. He was so sure about it that he decided to drive the two hours north and take the ferry to Great Morse Island to try and talk him into it.

Owen called Susannah from the island to tell her that they had recruited not only Kip Poucette, but he would be bringing two others from Richardson's. He explained one guy was named Neville Joseph, a West Indian shipwright from the island of St. Vincent and one other guy they called Mysterious Nick who had recently gotten out of the county jail. Owen explained that Nick had been in jail only a short time for "gardening," or growing copious amounts of marijuana which was still illegal in Maine. They would all arrive on Kip's boat in two or three days' time. Owen said he would sail down with them and get them settled. He would return later to get his car. Owen then said, "Tell everyone."

Their pending arrival marked the perfect chance to get townspeople excited as it had been seven decades since men had traveled to Ossonet to work in the shipyards. Susannah wrote a few short pieces for the blog, talked up the arrival of the workmen, and Bill at the *Clydebank News* asked Francis to stop by.

A few days later there was a small party of people at the town landing. They were awaiting the arrival of the new men with Owen on the high tide. Francis, Janet Gregory, who was there with her father, the rusticators, and a sullen Wes Martin, among others all stood milling about at the town landing, waiting for the boat. Janet asked Susannah, "So, who are these new recruits, anyway? My father keeps insisting this means that good shipbuilding jobs are coming back to town."

"Well, not exactly paying jobs, but they agreed to work on a kind of barter system," Susannah explained. "I see the boat now. They are rounding the bend."

Just then, Wes Martin walked over to Susannah and Janet and tapped Susannah on the shoulder rather sharply. "I hope this guy bringing a boat in isn't planning to stay long on my dock," pointing to Kip's boat as it came upriver.

Janet gave him an annoyed look and came to Susannah's side. "Your dock?" she asked. "This is the town dock."

"Yeah, and there is a one hour time limit for tie-up," Wes reminded them.

As the boat came closer, it was difficult not to admire its beauty. It was a forty-foot wooden yawl coming in under sail. Four men moved around the boat as it got closer, taking down the sails and coasting in on the current, preparing to hitch up to the dock. As they pulled up, those standing on shore got a look at the new shipwrights.

Not everyone was excited about their arrival.

"Owen Dodd is bringing in a bunch of new squatters who look like delegates from the United Nations," she heard Wes say to someone nearby.

They were indeed quite a motley-looking crew, a bit weathered after three days and two nights traveling by water. Owen's hair was sticking up in the air, and he had a stubbly beard and needed a shave. Kip was wearing the same French fur trapper hat and beaded coat, while Neville Joseph's sun-tipped dreadlocks and aviator sunglasses accentuated his brown skin and impressive goatee. Mysterious Nick was wearing a tan and tattered Carhartt jacket and wool navy cap and was smoking a cigarette. Kip was the first to disembark, and he walked toward Susannah and Janet to say hello. As Kip got closer to the two women, Janet nudged Susannah. "Isn't he a tall drink of water?"

Kip had native American ancestry, and with that red stocking cap, hand-carved tools, and beaded leather coat, he was intriguing. Neville and Mysterious Nick were next, and finally Owen jumped off and said a few words to the small crowd.

"We have a team of shipwrights, folks," he said and gestured towards Kip, Neville, and Mysterious Nick. "Finest kind."

The small gathering of locals sized up the men, mostly proud that at least they were here. Susannah knew from her studies with Eric that restoring traditions is key to any culture's survival, and it was part of Ossonet's long history to have skilled shipwrights coming to town to work in the shipyard. It was as old as the tradition of shipbuilding itself, and it turned out their arrival had more of an impact on changing people's minds about the historical importance of their river basin than the schooner itself. To see people coming to town to work at one of their native son's long-standing shipyards had begun changing people's minds about a marina project. After the shipwrights arrived, it seemed reading *Downriver with Dodd* reminded the old timers of this sense of pride and connection to the history of the river basin. Talk about it began all around town.

CHAPTER EIGHT

With three more men on hand, the framing process of the schooner began in earnest. A whirlwind kicked up at the Dodd shipyard and house. Kip was living nearby on his boat across the basin. Neville and Mysterious Nick were living rent free in one of the old Gregory buildings. They had no problem walking right up to the house and opening the door to get Owen. After working, they lingered in the shipyard with Owen, but she did not offer them dinner. Susannah missed those more easy-going summer days with just Owen. She got easily startled by them coming through the front door, and out in the shipyard she felt she was backing up into an unfamiliar piece of moving machinery every time the busy men tipped their hats to her as they worked. They did not speak to her directly at first.

The frames were coming together in the barn, after the men finished choosing scantlings and cutting futtocks. It was done with speed and accuracy, and there were no more clumsy volunteers or a girlfriend around trying to manage the large band saw with Owen, but it also meant Susannah never got to cut scantlings again. The futtocks would be cut and carried to the barn and laid out on the floor, stacking them two layers thick. The men would take turns hard- driving wooden nails into them. After the wooden nails, the bronze nails were drilled into the futtocks to complete the double-sawn frame. Traditional shipwrights believed that although wooden nails were very functional, a solid ship needed the strongest and most durable of metals too. The wooden nails would swell up and become watertight, but the rust-proof and expensive bronze nails could withstand immense pressure while underway.

The men from Great Morse Island brought energy, skill, and stamina to the Dodd yard. They had a short season when they could work for the love of the craft and not be paid. They were all very like minded, however, and Owen and the Great Morse Island men—as well as the rusticators who came by to help—were having a really good time working together and had developed a unique banter. Their jokes and laughter drew more local men over, men who had skills, to lend a hand as well when needed. Owen believed this kind of volunteering would last if they could keep it fast and fun.

The banter and laughter went on all day long. The men picked up on a specific bit of information that at first seemed awkward, and they would run with it. They joked and ribbed each other, but they also figured out problems and kept moving. Susannah observed that it was a way to work cooperatively and was intrigued by how it all went.

"You might have been right about the shape and length of the frame, Kip, but I never really loved you," Owen said while examining a piece of freshly cut wood.

"I never loved you, either, Owen, but I think the scantling was cut too short," Kip answered back. This had all started when Seb shared a story about a woman he once dated who broke it off with him. As an attempt to soften the blow, her parting words were, "I never really loved you anyway." The men had seized on its cruelty and spoke to everyone else this way for weeks.

"You will need an extra bronze screw on that futtock there, Nick," Kip would say minutes after Owen shared that he did not love him.

Mysterious Nick shrugged and said, "Maybe so, but I never really loved you anyway," which could be interpreted as "I am not sure I agree."

At this point, Neville might offer his opinion. "I think one more would do it," and this would prompt Kip to disagree once more, prompting Neville to say, "Mon, Kip, I never loved you."

Owen would then weigh in and say, "Got to say Neville is right on this one, Kip, but I never loved either of you anyway."

Hence, without argument or bad feelings, they kept pressing ahead with the work, weighing in on what should be done and then doing it. "Looking good!" Seb would say as he entered the yard to help with the work. "But I don't love you, Owen."

The pace really quickened with three skilled shipwrights working with Owen, and frames were now more consistently coming out of the barn door. There was a lot to blog about and "Frame up!" was now a common call in the working shipyard.

One of Susannah's main "jobs" was to call Janet Gregory and let her know anytime a frame was going up so Janet could drive her father over to see it. Mr. Gregory's excitement meant that on Frame Up days, he would have the car door open and one foot out on the ground before his daughter could park. As he struggled out of the car, she and Janet would help O.G keep his balance as he impatiently waited for one of them to get his walker. He would then make rapid, small steps toward the house, frustrated by any obstacles in his way, using the tennis balls at the bottom of his walker to plod through. Once inside he would skirt over to the porch, hitting a few pieces of furniture along the way, where he could then watch the frame go up. He was always dressed well for the occasion, wearing his tweed jacket, bow tie, and a porkpie hat. He would stand like a yard owner, nervous and pressed against the window where he stood waiting, tapping the glass lightly with his bony finger.

On this particularly cold afternoon, a very large frame was going up, so Janet and Susannah joined O.G., and they all gathered at the window to watch.

"Oh, that is a nice one," O.G. said as his nose was now pressing up against the window. "That should set things just right as that is a good, tall frame. Got to weigh about one thousand pounds. The ship looks 'bout framed to past midships now. He is more than halfway there."

They could hear Owen call out the two words that O.G. could hear loud and clear.

"FRAME UP!" Owen yelled as the old man took his hands off his walker and stood up straight. They watched as the men dropped what they were doing and walked over to the completed frame.

"FRAME UP!" Owen yelled.

They heaved it up high. O.G. watched with approval and exclaimed, "Finest kind!"

The three of them lingered by the window as the men secured the frame by driving bronze screws and metal bolts into the wooden part of the keel, using betels. It was fast work, and frame number thirty-five was up. As the men got back to what they had been working on, the banter started up again among the men.

"That looks like a good piece to use for the forward frames, but you see the knot?" Owen said to Kip.

"That is a slight check, not a knot, but if you say so," Kip agreed to disagree. "I wouldn't use this piece," he advised.

"I can't let a knot get in the way of a good futtock," Owen replied. "Knot this time."

"I am now twisted in knots, Owen!" Kip said, a bit exasperated. "And I don't love you."

"Just remember I never loved you, Kip." Owen had to yell above the wind. "You may be right, though. It is not a knot I want in a frame. What else you got?"

They both laughed as together they looked hard for a better piece.

"What are they talking about now?" the old man had heard the banter as they were not far from the house. He had thought he heard something about loving each other. "What was this about love?"

"They talk like this all the time," Susannah said reassuringly, and Janet was very amused. They watched and listened. It was easy to hear through the uninsulated walls of the house. Susannah explained it had all started because poor Seb had gotten his heart broken.

As Janet and her father readied to leave, Janet said to Susannah, "Poor old Seb—unlucky in love. He is probably in the right town for it. Full of old bachelors and spinsters."

Feeling a little stuck on the word spinster, Susannah said, "I could never think of you as a spinster."

"Around here I would say everyone is old before their time," Janet observed. "And not in a hurry to change."

O.G. wasn't really listening to the women folk but he did have an opinion about the men. It wasn't about love. It was about food.

"Got to bring 'em some hot food, girls," he said quite loudly with his finger pointing to the kitchen. He hobbled into the main room with his walker. "Got to feed them a meal. These men are hungry. Even if neither of you knows how to cook, it will taste good to them, and they are going to eat like a judgment."

"Dad!" Janet said. "I know how to cook."

"What?" her father said. "Not that diet stuff. These men need some real food."

"It's for your health, Dad," Janet sighed, getting ready to bring her dad home.

Susannah confessed to Janet that she wasn't sure what to do with the men coming and going from the house all the time or what to feed them.

"You aren't living here full time yet?" Janet asked.

"Not yet, but I think, or hope, it's going that way," she answered.

"Good," Janet said. "Well, my grandmother Gregory used to say to me when I was young, 'Dearie, there are two things you must never do for a happy life in a shipyard. Don't feed them and don't let 'em use the bathroom.' I guess she thought shipbuilding was going to last through my lifetime."

"Well, that is interesting! Wise words," Susannah said. "Unfortunately, they already use the bathroom."

"Got to feed 'em," Mr. Gregory piped in.

"Okay, Dad!" Janet said. She found it frustrating that her father had selective hearing. He could hear conversations that interested him, but when it came to his own health or taking his medicine, he never listened.

As they were leaving, Janet whispered to Susannah, "Don't let them take over the house! Do you know anything about them? What is the story with Kip? I bet Owen is trying to one up him a bit."

"That's what I told Owen," Susannah joked, "but he didn't seem to think that was very funny. Yet he is out there telling Kip he once loved him or never loved him, and he hardly knows the guy!" The two women could banter too.

"Now, what about this Kip guy?" Janet asked.

Susannah had learned a bit more about Kip. She had discovered a little news story about Great Morse Island in a coastal Maine magazine. Over the past two centuries, his island had become an artist's colony, as Maine islands and coasts have always been important to artists like Andrew Wyeth, Edward Hopper, Rockwell Kent, and Winslow Homer. Great artists have often mingled among the locals in Maine, and on Great Morse Island, one of its summer residents included one of North America's premiere landscape artists, Arthur Twinton.

The article featured a unique story about a young man whose

mother, a native of the Micmac tribe that once lived throughout the coast of Maine, had apprenticed at the local boat shop with master shipwright Samuel Richardson. However, artist Arthur Twinton was a friend and neighbor, and Kip had helped him with odd jobs at the studio since he was a kid. Under the guidance of Arthur Twinton and Samuel Richardson, Kip's talent at both fine art and woodworking had been encouraged and nurtured by his two mentors. Susannah wondered if this was why Kip seemed to have a sensitivity and reserve that Owen simply did not have. It was perhaps the fine artist in him. She wasn't sure.

In the article, there was a quote from Mr. Richardson that said, "Kip apprenticed with me as a youth, and from the get-go I was so impressed with his joinery work. That is a talent. He didn't learn watercolors from me, though!" There was a photo in the article of a landscape painting of Great Morse Island by Kip. It turns out, Twinton urged Kip to apply for scholarships, and he then attended Pratt Institute in New York City. As Susannah did more research, she learned Kip did spend time in New York, with several gallery shows. Susannah wondered if this might explain how he could afford to work on the schooner without pay. She relayed the story to Janet, who was also very impressed that someone so talented chose to come to Ossonet.

"It would be great if he could paint some of this," Janet said. "Maybe he could paint something I could give to my dad."

As they walked back to the car, Owen and the men stopped working, and out of respect they all waved to Mr. Gregory.

"Nice work, boys!" he shouted to them. "Finest kind."

Owen gave a big wave and a nod to Janet. Janet also waved to them. "I'll always love you!"

"I'll always love you too, Janet!" Owen yelled. He shrugged. "Oops!"

He walked over to Susannah and said, "Sorry about that."

Susannah bantered back, "Isn't she like your second cousin anyhow?"

"Probably." Owen was flashing his green eyes at her. "Glad you all still love me though."

CHAPTER NINE

Maine's harvest season had already gone by, so the bushel of shiny Macintosh apples that they kept refilling for the shipwrights to snack on all fall was down to the bottom, and it was mostly mushy pulp. While working outside was invigorating in October, it was a lot different now that it was mid-November. Still planking, still building frames, the wind from the river was cold and damp; after they carried out frames from the barn and lifted them onto the schooner, they often scurried back to the woodstove in the barn loft to get a bit of warmth.

Each morning, Owen would say, "Got to start feeding the men," and he would open and close the empty kitchen cabinets. She usually spotted him trying to open a can of sardines or some potato chips.

"Sardines again, Owen?" Susannah hated the smell. "Why not get them some hot dogs?"

"Can you pick some up in Clydebank?" he asked. "I'll pay you back."

It was the time of year in Maine when people made stews or served hot meals with freshly harvested fingerling potatoes, brussels sprouts, or squash from the farmers' market. What they were offering the hardworking shipwrights was cheap and meager. While Susannah had been enjoying this time of year and had gotten familiar with the many farms and markets in the region, she had no cooking skills of her own. Learning to cook might lead to feeding the men, so in buying hot dogs, cans of soup, or sardines she could still heed Janet Gregory's grandmother's words not to let the men in the house. She was worried they would start coming in at all hours, or she would have to spend her time constantly competing with four or five men for Owen's attention. Yet each time another frame went on that schooner and the men had done another beautiful job with it, Mr. Gregory's words that you "got to feed them" ran through her mind. Their living arrangements were cold enough, with Kip living on his boat while Neville and Mysterious Nick were heating the ramshackle house they were living in with wood. Kip was often rubbing his hands with the cold after a night sleeping on his boat, and Neville talked more and more about missing his warm Caribbean Island of St. Vincent. Mysterious Nick was seemingly smoking more cigarettes for warmth. They were working for free, for the experience of learning how to construct a double-sawn oak schooner, but it could not last if they did not do something. She had managed to get permission to work from home more often, so she was often in Ossonet, at the big table near the window of the main room watching them work. As the temperatures dropped more and more, she finally couldn't bear it. She could not stand watching them freeze outside and huddle in the loft any longer. Finally, she said to Owen, "Let them in."

"It's high time we get this thing going," Owen said, and looked relieved and grateful. "Got to have mug up around 10:30 a.m. and got to give them hot food for lunch," he told Susannah.

"Owen, I can reheat stuff, but I don't really know how to cook. I don't really have time."

"I'll take care of lunch if you do mug up," he offered.

He instructed her to pick up some donuts or bagels and coffee, with her own money apparently, and try to be home to make the coffee. She was instructed to ring the ship's bell outside the door each day she was there and yell, "Mug up!"

"Just make sure the coffee is hot," he advised. "Oh, and I will pay you back for sure on that," he explained, "but mug up is huge. We need the break, and we need to talk about the work."

"And what's in it for me?" she teased, half joking but also a little put out.

"You can blog about it, right?" Owen said. "Oh, one problem is we are going to have to wash all the mugs. Hang them on a rack so every mug up everyone has a clean mug."

"Just like being at a youth hostel," Susannah muttered.

"Or a hotel!" Owen added, thinking she was delighted with the idea of washing up after them.

Although Owen said he would take care of lunch, he was trying to figure out how to do it cheaply. He said, "I can buy a bushel of clams each week from the shell fishermen and just add onions for variety. I can vary the menu with the occasional chicken pot pie. We need something filling like hand pie," he noted.

"No broths."

They had a very limited budget, as Owen was scraping by on his savings to pay for the materials for the boat, and Susannah was reluctant to part with her weekly paycheck on food for five or six men. So, local clam chowder and hand pies were going to be the main fare. She figured they would enjoy whatever was put down in front of them. But she was pleasantly surprised by what happened next.

After a couple of weeks of Susannah's meager offerings and Owen's watery chowders, it was Kip who first "came out" as a bona fide foodie.

Kip grew up eating French, Canadian, and Micmac cuisine, which revolved around fresh seafood, but he had also lived in New York and had friends in the restaurant business, so he figured his skills in the culinary arts might be a welcome change by now.

"Got some lobster traps dangling right off my boat, and I could haul them up," he told them all at lunch. "If you provide the butter, Susannah, I'll prepare you lobster thermidor with *bechamel* coated lobster. *Ce sera délicieux.*"

The room was silent at first, but Kip explained.

"On Great Morse Island, we substitute scalloped potatoes for mashed potatoes and peas. The butter will provide the base for my sauce," he noted. Susannah had not realized that he spoke French.

A few days later, Kip brought his ingredients and prepared them what felt like a Thanksgiving feast. The time Kip put into it merited Susannah taking pictures of them at the table digging in. She decided to write about the lobster thermidor for the blog, and she got hundreds of comments praising the food. Soon after, Mysterious Nick also came out as a Cajun of sorts and offered to cook a rappie pie for them, the French Acadian dish favored in Nova Scotia that is a mix of potatoes and chicken. The French and Acadian influence on cooking in the Maritimes permeated many of the foods Nick and Kip talked about, including Cajun dishes from Louisiana. Nick explained the story of the expulsions of the Acadian French to the shores of Louisiana in the 1700s where they became known as Cajuns. Kip had traveled and lived in France and had once been intimately involved with a French woman, and they were always cooking together. Kip and Mysterious Nick's French, Cajun and Acadian food, including a coquille Saint Jacques sandwich, prompted them to ask Owen if he could get them some scallops. With Kip's help, Nick stunned them all when he served gourmet poached scallops in a creamy white wine sauce.

Susannah photographed all the dishes and did a little research on the regions they came from. She wrote about the meals in *Downriver with Dodd*, and the interest among nearby Maine cooks began to grow. When it was Neville's turn to showcase his culture's West Indian cooking, she documented his homemade Jamaican jerk pork and Caribbean garlic mashed potatoes with okra and fried plantains and explained they washed it down with just a small shot of rum. Readers so enjoyed hearing about Neville's grilled chicken, johnnycake, and rib-covering bread pudding, along with the cuisine of the maritime cooks, Kip and Nick, that they could not be outdone and began emailing over their own recipes. It was like a test kitchen; they could then thank whoever sent the recipes and take a photo of the result when they found time to get all the ingredients. It seems a good cook prefers to showcase their own work, so one morning, Susannah opened the front door and found a large cooking pan full of fish cakes, lightly seasoned with breadcrumbs and fresh onions. There was a note that said, "Heat at 350 degrees for twenty minutes. Also warm up the brown bread. Use plenty of butter while it's hot." Soon, homemade baked beans became a staple, and pots would get dropped off sometimes twice a week. The generous chef who had baked them would come by to pick up the pot and say, "Mine's the one with the slightly cracked handle. I know it anywhere as my son knocked it off the table and cracked it when he was a boy." And of course this was thirty-five years ago. No self-respecting Maine cook would ever dream of getting a new beanpot— they were passed down by each generation and were full of memories, not just salt pork and molasses.

After all this great eating, Susannah thought her editor might enjoy a story about all this. Not just a culinary point of view, it was really about the people of the county and how generous they were.

Bill missed the point, unfortunately. "Francis will be managing the bigger stories about the schooner, and besides, the best cooks in Maine are certainly not in Ossonet," he presumed. "The best chefs tend to be in Portland where there is more of an interest and appreciation of the culinary arts."

As more frames went up, more pots of beans, delicious whoopie pies, fish cakes, buttered brown bread, *tourtière*—a French-Canadian meat pie that was brought to Maine by the French-speaking mill workers of the eighteenth and nineteenth centuries—and numerous casseroles fed the men of the Dodd shipyard as a show of support for reviving the shipyard and building a schooner. For those who did not cook, they were happy to put donations in a jar to buy coffee or breakfast items for mug ups.

She once again tried to explain it all to her boss and said, "It's really about the people, their history and the food that influenced it all. This is one of the most unique things I have ever experienced, and it is like a revival of traditions, stories, and the whole community is taking part."

"That is all well and good," Bill said, "but just remember, Susannah, people bringing food to a house is not news. We are a local newspaper, and we do tend to publish more nuts-and-bolts stories, less fluff."

"But this fluff is going to get a schooner framed by Christmas," she insisted.

Bill finally decided to send Francis to Ossonet to see what was for lunch. Upon his return, Francis apparently told him that there was nothing remarkable about the fish cakes. They were dry. What he didn't tell him is they were prepared by a ninety-two-year-old Ossonet lady who grew up near the shipyard. She, too, recalled the days when the shipyard was alive with activity. She had made her fish cakes at the urging of her grandson who had brought them over that morning. They were dry, but their flavor was not lost on any of them, except the *Clydebank News*.

CHAPTER TEN

While it was relatively quiet in and around the Dodd and Gregory yards at night, most of the time Owen was in the barn mapping out the next day's work and where planks would go. He enjoyed the quiet of the barn loft and usually lost track of time up there.

On this evening, the local weather mentioned that high winds were expected, and because of an astronomically high tide, would cause coastal flooding. Owen was in the loft and had the music station playing on the radio. The work was absorbing, and he didn't notice the weather and had forgotten about the astronomical tide. A tide like that can strand anyone in the barn, which was built on stilts overhanging the river. And before too long the path between the schooner and the barn was full of water, making it impossible to cross on foot.

Susannah could see from the house the tide rising much faster than usual. It was like a gush of water came in very fast and was surrounding the building area of the schooner.

Around ten o'clock she looked out the window again and at first thought she was staring at accumulating snow. But it was in fact whitecaps which were flooding in and across the shipyard. In the dark night, she thought she saw pieces of wood and stray construction materials floating in the water. She had not been informed by Owen that the shipyard floods during a storm and wondered whether she should try to save the construction materials. She wanted to call Owen on his mobile phone, but a transformer had gone down and must have knocked out cell service. Because he was a "mar'ster hand" according to the local description of Owen, meaning a master craftsman and skilled at so many things that she simply couldn't do, he had given her only rather abrupt explanations of how things worked around the shipyard. Right now, she really needed to be decisive. She went outside with a flashlight and started shouting.

"Water is up to the barn!" she shouted, gesturing broadly at the water that now separated them. "Water is around the schooner!" Owen finally came to the loft window.

"Stay there!" he shouted, gesturing that she steer clear of the rising water near the schooner and the barn. "Don't go any farther! Be in when it goes down a bit!" He didn't seem to register how the tide had just turned and would continue to rise. Susannah headed back inside. Knowing that he was somewhat stranded, he planned to use the lightweight rowboat that was stowed in the barn to get across the high water to the house. He'd done it hundreds of times before when the shipyard had flooded during a full moon tide. He had no concerns that he could not get across in the dark and it was simply the method the Dodds had always used to cross over.

He soon finished up work and got ready to row over towards the house. As Owen prepared to take the lightweight rowboat, he meant to grab an oar so he could propel himself the short distance across to the high ground just ten yards away. He distractedly grabbed a large broom that was leaning against the barn door, thinking it was his oar. He had expertly plopped down in the boat and shoved off from the barn in hopes of propelling himself quickly across the short distance as he often did, when he realized he had a broom, not an oar. He saw his mistake at the same time the storm current and peak high tide were changing. This had caused waves to pile up on one another and increase in size, while the whirlpool was churning faster than ever. He knew instantly that he had made a major miscalculation. His little lightweight dory quickly got sucked away from the barn by the force of the rushing water. The broom was useless, and he was essentially rudderless. He was unable to wrestle with the strength of the outgoing tide and currents or the force of the wind with his barn broom and tippy boat.

He tried frantically paddling with his broom, then with both arms, but the little boat was quickly swept out beyond the dock into the basin, being carried quickly with the current.

Moments before, Susannah had found the flashlight and was

going to check on the building materials and see what was floating away. Although he had not explained it very well, she realized that Owen would wait out the high tide in the barn, but he had instead been keen to get across to the house. She looked out to see the lights were now off in the loft, but there was no sign of Owen.

She scanned the area with her flashlight, and to her horror, she watched as Owen was swept away from the barn trying in vain to use the broom to paddle against the storm. She could now see the little boat was being pulled toward the dark waters of the river basin, where the wind and current had whipped the whirlpool into an angry boil. Horrified, she was convinced Owen would disappear into that vortex. She shouted for him, but Owen could not hear her. She thought she heard him yell "Help!"

Owen had indeed called for help and was beginning to panic as he knew he was being swept closer to the whirlpool which would not swallow him up but would likely capsize him. The water was frigid, and he was not a strong swimmer. He calculated he might be better off drifting out to the open waters during a North Atlantic gale. Realizing this was his option, he had in fact yelled for help and hoped one of the rusticators would hear him, as they would know what to do.

Susannah thought of only one person who was strong and quick enough to save Owen, so she ran along the shore and over the creek bridge in the direction of Kip's boat where she saw a light on. The rest of the town was dark from the power outage. She could see just a speck of Owen making some progress, paddling with the broom away from the whirlpool while fighting the strong currents that were dragging him farther out.

Susannah reached Kip's boat.

"Kip!" She jumped onto the deck of his boat from the dock in one leap.

"Owen's out there!" she pointed, out of breath, towards the darkness. "Owen is in trouble out there!" Kip scrambled up from his cabin. It seemed he might have heard Owen as well as he looked like he was already putting on his foul weather gear.

She remembered there was a long boat tied up near the town landing. It was used if someone needed to make a water rescue and belonged to the town. They had both passed by it many times. "The rescue boat!" she shouted, and then "Grab that oar!" and he yanked the oar that was tied down to his own boat and they rushed towards the long boat. It was their best chance of reaching him before it was too late, but Kip wondered if Susannah should be going out there.

She was already in the boat, and it had two oars, so she was ready to go. Susannah shouted. "Get in, Kip!" She prayed it was seaworthy.

She was planning to go after Owen with or without Kip, but Kip had no intention of letting her go out there alone. Kip pushed off the boat and lost his footing, but he held on. She already had the two oars in their oarlocks and so she immediately started to row toward Owen as Kip hauled himself up and over the stern and began to propel, steer and steady the boat with his oar. They were now moving quickly, and as they got closer to Owen, Susannah tried a sudden turn towards him and then shouted a command of "Steer!"

Kip used his oar like a rudder. Owen's boat was being pulled farther out to the edge of the whirlpool when they finally caught up to him.

Owen had stopped trying to row with his useless broom. He was wet and his bare hands were gripping the sides of the small boat to keep it stable. He was numb and cold and unable to do much more than crouch down in the center of the little boat and just go in a strange, eerie ride farther out towards the bay. The boat was starting to take on water and become less and less stable. He was near the point of being swamped when he heard a woman's voice yelling his name.

Susannah yelled, "Hard left!" to Kip who turned the boat hard to port. Kip threw his full weight into turning the boat with his oar as he crouched in the stern.

Owen could not see any land in sight as he peered over the side of his sinking boat. A sense of panic was setting in and already affecting Owen's thoughts, and in his altered state he thought he saw a Viking woman, larger than life, coming through a roaring storm in full command of the situation. His thought was "Who is that?"

"Owen, jump in. Jump!" Kip shouted as he was approaching the boat alongside.

"Owen!" she shouted. "Get in!"

He snapped out of it. "Get closer, Kip!" She gave two last long strokes, her arms burning, and as their long boat shot forward, she pulled her oar in so it would not knock Owen, now standing up in his boat, over, preparing to jump. Kip steered them close enough alongside

Owen that he was able to literally leap, drop, and roll into the long boat as his small dory swamped and was then swept down into the whirlpool out of sight. Owen landed hard but Susannah had not once let go of her oars. She now struggled to row three people back towards shore as the tide and wind were against them. Kip had abandoned his position and had one hand on Owen. "Stay there," Kip ordered Owen not to move as he did not want more movement which would swamp the boat. It had a lot of water in it now but there was no time to bail. Kip sat next to Susannah and took an oar. "Two, Six Heave!" he said, and they powered the boat together. They pulled hard through the water— in synch—and against the odds, they got the boat moving in the right direction. Owen had not moved from the spot where he'd landed. He felt so relieved and grateful as he watched his rescuers pulling on their oars separately but essentially rowing as one. Owen was in shock but felt certain that these two people, who he still didn't quite realize were Susannah and Kip, would get him to shore. He could see them rowing madly and was still convinced he was being rescued by a couple of Vikings.

They finally got within a few yards of the shore. They could see some flashlights on the beach and steered towards them.

Finally, they all heard the gravelly bottom. They were nearly ashore.

Seb, Neville, and the rusticators had heard the yelling for Owen on the river, and when they saw the rescue boat was gone, they were all feeling a bit helpless, standing along the shore, hoping to see their friends again. As the long boat finally reached the land, the men rushed in and helped pull the boat ashore. Owen hadn't moved from his kneeling position, and even with him still in it they dragged the boat up even farther on to the dry land to be sure everyone got out safely. They helped Owen get out, and seeing how frozen he was they led him quickly towards the shanties where a woodstove was going. Seb was a little shocked at how pale Owen looked as he walked him towards the warm shed. "Owen, you look death struck."

"I'm okay," a relieved and shivering Owen said as they all left the boat and hurried towards shelter. "I think I was rescued by a couple of Vikings."

"About right," Seb agreed. "They did good."

"Just going to get my dory tomorrow," Owen said feebly.

"Forget about it," Seb said. "With that wind blowing all hell out by the roots, you may not find her."

"Got a fire going. You all need to get warm now." It was smart to get him inside quickly. He had not been wearing his thick coat or a hat. He needed the warmth of the fire and was too close to hypothermia to venture all the way back to his own house. They got him some whiskey and he drank that while taking off his sweater, boots, and socks. Seb gave Owen some old dry work clothes to put on and he started to warm up.

Susannah and Kip followed behind, frozen themselves as the adrenaline waned. When they entered the shack, it was still dark because of the power outages so a kerosene lamp had been lit. They would fix them all right up, Seb said, who was now boiling water, and started pouring hot coffee with plenty of whiskey in it for three mugs.

"You okay?" Kip asked Owen. "You look a bit wet and sozzled."

"Yeah, I'm good. You?"

"I'm good." The two men exchanged a few more words, and the rusticators were quiet. Susannah put her hand on Owen's shoulder, "You okay?"

He nodded, "Yes. Thank you."

They stayed on near the stove. They all got quite drunk as they rehashed what happened, how it happened, and who was doing what when it happened. Owen remained in the chair with two blankets over him while Susannah and Kip shared a bench and were covered with the same blanket. At one point, they nearly tipped the bench and had to hold onto each other to regain their balance. No one seemed to notice. They all agreed that they should remain silent and neither the harbormaster nor the cops—nor other rusticators either—should know about this. Finally, the storm had subsided, and their clothes were dry. The night air was calm enough to get back to the Dodd house without freezing.

Owen had a hot shower, and they spent another hour talking in bed.

"You should NOT have gone out on the river like that," he scolded her. "You don't have the experience!" If a newcomer like Susannah had drowned while rescuing a waterman from Ossonet, Owen was correct in feeling that he would be squarely to blame.

Susannah, oddly, was feeling powerful and completely sure of herself. It was a new feeling for her. "I couldn't let you be swept out to sea. I got Kip. Between us, we did the right thing. I felt safe with him steering the boat and it meant I could keep an eye on you. We got to you quickly, thanks to him really."

"Why didn't you get Seb?' Owen asked.

"We needed Kip," she said.

He was worn out. She had put lots of blankets on top of him. He finally fell asleep.

She tossed and turned and could not quite process all that had happened and why from that night on she felt different. She knew she did the right thing calling for Kip's help. She finally slept and dreamed that it was summer, and the water was calm. She had crossed the yard to Kip's boat. In the dream he had the radio on, and it was playing 1920s jazz tunes. She had never seen the interior of his boat, but in the dream she saw it had gracefully curved gunnels running from the deck to the keel through the cabin. The gunnels were beautifully varnished. The main cabin had a thick oak table. In the dream, a swinging kerosene lamp was lit. It was suspended from the cabin ceiling and gave the wooden cabin a soft, polished glow. Beneath the galley stove, there was a small cast iron woodstove that Kip used for both heating and cooking. In the dream Susannah could see the flames inside the cast iron door.

She sat down on the shiny cabin bench, while Kip stoked the stove and added a piece of wood. The kettle on the stove was steaming and he was readying mugs for tea.

"My father always said you must add something nutritious to tea," he said thoughtfully. "This ginger is the best for any ailment."

"And what do you think ails me?" she asked him in the dream.

Kip handed her the mug, and instead it was a carved owl made of soapstone that fit comfortably in her palm.

She looked up, and it was not Kip but a tall woman standing there. Susannah knew without asking that she was a native American woman, and somehow guessed she was a member of one of the Greenland tribes. The woman came up to her and touched her arm, pointing to what was now the mug of tea in her hand. The woman said, "You have a *kaffemik*?" Susannah knew that in Greenland the word means a kind of social gathering. Susannah nodded yes. The woman turned away and then turned back and handed her something like ginger root as they did in Laos. But as she looked at her, the woman's face had changed from a human face into the face of an owl.

As the dream was ending, before waking up, Susannah said, "I am braver than I thought." And awoke with those words repeating themselves in her mind.

The next day she remembered the dream clearly and was puzzled by it, a little groggy from all the whiskey and the very real adventure on the river the night before. A few days later, she found a newly made wooden oar leaning against the house near the front door. Susannah thought for sure it was a gift from Owen for helping him on the river. But when she asked him, he said, "No, I am sorry I am too busy to make an oar." She looked closely at its smooth handle and feathered paddle and thought she would keep it by the barn door in case Owen or anyone else ever needed it. She saw Kip later in the day, and standing in the dooryard, said, "Did you bring by that oar for Owen?" and he said, "No, it's for you. The paddle is a very important symbol to Micmac people. Maybe it will remind you of your bravery."

She was startled by what he said and asked, "Do you know anything about spirit animals? I saw a woman turn into an owl in a dream."

"A spirit animal can be anything you want," Kip said. "Where were you when you saw the woman?"

She hesitated to tell him but hoped it also might solve the puzzle.

"I was in the cabin of your boat. An owl served me a cup of hot, milky coffee."

He paused and leaned into the dooryard, kicking a bit of snow. "I am no visionary, but a spirit animal can transform you into something or someone else. That is just my interpretation! Transformation is the main thing to think of."

"Oh, and thank you for the oar."

"A spare oar always comes in handy," he said. Just then, Owen came to the dooryard and waved to Kip.

"Thanks, man," he went outside and shook Kip's hand.

"Glad you are okay," Kip said, and they gave each other a quick hug and slap on the back. Feeling a bit overwhelmed by what almost happened on the water the night before, Susannah said, "Can I get in there?" and came outside to give them both a hug.

CHAPTER ELEVEN

Owen had followed a tradition in any large construction project of using a "topping tree" to mark and eventually celebrate the completion of the skeleton of a building structure. He had lashed a small Douglas fir tree to the top of the bare stem post at the front of the unfinished schooner so tightly that it had stayed true despite the December weather. In keeping with the season, Owen had shimmied up the stern post and strung a few lights around the topping tree and used two industrial strength extension cords long enough to keep the holiday lights plugged in. Before bed each night, Susannah and Owen stood at the window looking out at the brave little tree hovering above the frames. Susannah felt a kinship to this little tree. Readers of the blog enjoyed it too. They commented, and she posted photos of the little tree and delved into the symbolism of trees, mentioning that a living tree can be a symbol of physical and spiritual nourishment, transformation, and liberation, even union and fertility. In the case of the schooner and the topping tree, they were also a symbol of sorts to everyone in Ossonet. A connection to the past, hope for the town and the community. The readers loved it.

In quiet moments, Susannah found herself dwelling on the river incident, but Owen would not speak of it, and neither would the rusticators. She had longed to share the story with someone, but it would risk shutting down the whole project if word got into the wrong hands.

Despite her uneasiness that something else might happen, like another accident or worse, during the week before December twenty-first, Owen informed her that "The topping tree will come down the minute we get the last frame up. You can mention it in your blog. We are going to have to light the tree to celebrate."

"Isn't it already lit?" she asked.

"Got to burn it," he answered. "You know how we like to burn things in Ossonet."

She had a vision of the framed hull catching fire and burning up like the piano did. As she got more nervous, he got more excited about his plan. "Got to get that last goddamn frame on this week and have a tree lighting. Got to get some folks down here to watch it and have a shindig."

"But we don't have to burn the place down," Susannah noted.

Oddly, Owen's Maine accent was getting thicker and more noticeable as time went on with the schooner project, and he often spoke in short, action-oriented sentences, saying, "Got to this" and "Got to that" with a peppering of "goddamn this" and "goddamn that."

"There is nothing to worry about on this," he assured her. "Not a goddamn thing."

When it came to that "goddamn last frame," they were nearly ready for the next step, the planking, and Susannah had not worked on the actual boat since that one day she cut the first futtocks at the band saw with Owen. Since the shipwrights had arrived, she had not touched a tool or a piece of wood. A young neighbor, sixteen-year-old Quinn Porter, had also joined the shipwrights every day after high school, so between them and the rusticators coming and going, the yard was always busy with men of all ages, laughing, working together, figuring out problems. She was writing about it and supportive of it and literally keeping the home fires burning. She was helping, but Susannah was starting to feel a little bit left out, like a boat widow, steadily losing ground to Owen's mistress—the schooner and its builders.

Owen did give her lots of jobs, and her most important job this day was to host a party at the Dodd house. She assumed that he would host it with her. They decided to make it a Frame Up and solstice party. They knew by now that people would bring lots of food. They just needed to provide some entertainment.

"I got that covered," Owen assured her.

She did not have to look too far to find the "fixings" for a shipyard party. She found a massive punch bowl in the attic; it looked like it had not been used since the 1950s. She also found folding chairs, ones that might fit around the main room "when company comes," and which she dusted, cleaned, and buffed. She found some old Christmas decorations stored in a box that had no sentimental value to her, but Owen got a kick out of seeing them again.

She bought a Christmas tree in Clydebank—and had delayed this hoping that Owen would go with her to the woods and cut one himself, but he didn't have time. She decorated the tree and lined the mantelpiece with pine boughs and hung some mistletoe above the front door. The first time Owen walked in after she'd hung it, she rushed over and made him stand under it where she pointed it out, hoping he would kiss her. He'd been in a rush and gave her a quick kiss. His lips were so dry and chapped from working outside that she commented, "You could sand the boat with those lips," as he dashed into the other room. He shot back, "Sand your bottom, did you say?"

The solstice party, as they now called it, would mark the first time in her life that Susannah would act as the hostess at a holiday party. It was not her home, but apparently as "the woman of the house," as Owen called her, she had to step up. She had to admit, despite his Maine-isms and the old-fashioned expectations, Susannah was both excited and a little nervous to host a party with her man, her main squeeze, her soon to be fiancé?

It was premature and silly, but she unwittingly got caught up in the idea of getting a "special" Christmas gift, maybe even an engagement ring.

On the day of the solstice party, it started to snow and by late afternoon it was getting heavier. As the men worked in the barn to finish putting together the final frame, Susannah had told local people to come when it got dark, so they began to arrive by snowshoe or cross-country skis, dragging their supply of beer or contribution to the table along with them on sleds or stuffed into backpacks.

Others parked near the old Gregory yard and struggled up the road to the Dodd house, lugging large lasagna pans or casserole dishes. They crossed over the icy creek bridge, passing the barn and the schooner, and entered the house in near collapse, adding their food offerings to the dining room table.

The shipwrights had also gotten into the party spirit. Earlier in the day, Neville had come by with his Caribbean-style Christmas rum cake for the table. Like many from the West Indies, Neville was influenced by his Protestant Adventist upbringing, but as a younger man, adopted a Rastafarian outlook. The combination meant Neville tended to be very open and giving and liked to bless the things he offered, like the rum cake which Susannah accepted graciously, now knowing how to respond to the gesture.

"Thank you, Nev. God bless you," she said.

"*Me'si,*" Neville said, "and you. Cheese-on-Bread! Wow! This place looks beautiful."

"Thank you, Nev," she said. He was relaxed and in a festive mood too.

Kip had been busy in the barn working on the last frame, but he had taken time to make a large bowl of Native American bean and corn succotash, while Mysterious Nick delivered creton, a French-Canadian meat spread or pâté. They all added something of their own heritage to the party.

Soon, the house and yard were packed with people. Susannah was pleased to see a familiar face among them when Janet Gregory arrived. She'd also brought a covered dish but was slipping a bit on the driveway, nearly losing her balance. Susannah ran out to help her.

"Hey," Susannah said. "Glad you could make it!"

"My father wants me to take pictures of the last frame going up," Janet said. "I wish he could be here, but with the snow, I was worried he might fall." They shared a guilty look as they were in fact relieved that he wasn't there. "He will be missed," Susannah said diplomatically. "I guess I should have let him come," Janet said unconvincingly.

Janet naturally assumed some of the hostess duties and greeted people she had known all her life, introducing them to Susannah. There were nearly thirty people inside and many more outside looking around at the half-finished ship. The next hour was a blur as Susannah and Janet rushed around making sure everyone had what they needed to enjoy the growing potluck spread. It was fun to work together and move about the kitchen with another woman; it reminded Susannah of the many holidays she spent with her mother and sisters getting ready for the relatives.

Meanwhile, Janet seemed to direct all the credit on her new friend. Susannah was fussed over and complimented by all the local women. They offered to help arrange the food, they mentioned to her how nice the house looked, and they treated it like it was her home, not just Owen's. It made Susannah feel very house-proud, and they made her feel like she belonged in this community.

All the chatter suddenly stopped as Owen came charging across the shipyard to the front door of the house and rang the big brass bell to get everyone's attention. He looked surprised to see so many people in and around the house. He waved hello to Susannah and kept ringing the bell, shouting, "Frame's going up! Last frame's going *up!*"

Those who were inside quickly put on their coats and joined the outside revelers. They all huddled in front of the house, watching the shipwrights carry the frame out of the barn and across the snowy yard toward the vessel.

The last frame was smaller in size as it would fit right up front, just below the topping tree. The men had set up a pulley to help lower the last frame in, yet symbolically the final frame's fitting into place was always described as going up.

Owen had told young Quinn to squeeze through the frames to get inside the skeleton of the vessel to help position the piece.

"FRAME UP!" Owen yelled for the last time, and the men heaved the frame up high with the pulley, then lowered it down as Owen guided it into place. Owen then clamored over Quinn and shimmied as high as he could above the framed ship to lift his sledgehammer high over his head and bring it down on the frame to drive the bolt in to the keel.

"Made!" Owen yelled, meaning it was completed. "*Made!*"

To everyone's surprise, instead of climbing down, Owen shimmied farther up the front stem of the ship and grabbed hold of the topping tree lashed to the ship's bow. He had told Quinn to hand him a tool from where Quinn stood, his neck straining as Owen was very high up at this point. Quinn handed him a crowbar. He quickly pried the small tree from where it was bolted down and unwound the Christmas lights to get them quickly off the tree, struggling to keep the tree upright as he did so.

"Quinn, get me the gasoline!" he yelled from up high above the ground. He steadied himself on the edge of the frame.

He was positioned just above Quinn, who had also been instructed to get him a lighter. Owen doused the tree.

"Get down, Quinn. Get away from the boat," Owen said, wanting Quinn out of harm's way, and Quinn clambered down the ribs of the ship like a fast-moving spider to the ground. As the tree started to tip toward the ground eighteen feet below, Owen ignited it with a lighter.

"Topping tree coming down!" Owen shouted.

The tree burst into a ball of flames at the same time Owen used all his strength to toss it high and away from the vessel while it burned. Like a meteor against the night sky, it blazed spectacularly for the few seconds before it hit the ground. The flames against the darkest night of the year were a purely pagan act, and everyone loved it.

When the burning tree reached the snowy ground, it sizzled, and the flames died down. Seb ran up with a small blowtorch and reignited it. Its branches crackled with the sound of dry kindling. The heathen-like ritual added to a celebratory and raucous mood among the guests.

Owen then shimmied down the frames and got his first look at a full schooner in frame. He forced back a lump rising in his throat marking a kind of victory for all of them. This was the first time in most of their lives that a schooner was in full frame in Ossonet instead of something they just saw photos of or talked about with the old timers. The moment was not lost on the townspeople, and the shipbuilding crew was soon surrounded by a crush of people from around the county, eager to shake their hands and congratulate them. People circled the beautiful ribs of the vessel, taking their time to admire the completed frames and the schooner's evolving shape.

Owen was so busy being celebrated, it took him a long while to come over to where Susannah was standing. He was followed by a woman who looked to be in her thirties also. "This is Sherry. And this is my girlfriend, Susannah," and he pointed to Susannah.

She shook Susannah's hand. She then added, "You've made my town and my old friend famous!" she said. "I read *Downriver with Dodd*. Great work."

Owen grabbed some bags of chips and a plate of hand pies someone had brought, and just as Susannah turned around to show someone where to put their coat, she watched Sherry and Owen head back out, and in their wake, a few other folks followed their lead and went back to the barn. Susannah was stung by the sudden appearance of this old friend of his while she was still left with so many people still in the house that she really didn't know. Susannah was glad Janet was still there.

"All the good Ossonet parties end up in a barn," Janet noted to reassure Susannah.

"Should I be worried?" asked Susannah.

Janet hesitated a moment and then said, "No," in a very matter-of-fact way. "It's more that most Dodds really can't handle alcohol very well especially at a big shindig. . . but otherwise, no. They are loyal."

"I just can't believe he blew me off that way, though."

In fact, she was a little shaken up by it.

"I think the whole town is excited," Janet reassured her. "Everyone has come home for Christmas, so they come out of the woodwork anyhow and then the schooner was the talk of the town. Sherry has been living away, I think, and is just back for the holiday. Nothing to worry about."

As the night went on, it seemed the late arrivals to the tree lighting ceremony just assumed the party was in the barn, so the house was a little empty as the well-fed guests inside the house had seen and heard the growing party in the barn and didn't want to miss out. It was still snowing, and the solstice night had brought in another astronomically high tide. Not long after the house had emptied out, Susannah decided to go to the barn, too. As she walked over, she realized the tide had now come in so high that the barn was cut off and again surrounded by icy cold water. Frightened by the rising river, she sternly warned the other stragglers that they would have to wait for the tide to recede. It had started to snow quite hard, so for a while everyone needed to stay put in the house and away from the barn.

Since most of the rusticators and the shipwrights ended up stranded in the barn, they were having their own rowdy shindig there. Soon the people inside the house could hear them singing sea shanties quite loudly, and Susannah could hear Owen's bellowing voice loudest of all:

Oh, molasses
He works in the sun, and he works in the rain.
Oh, molasses rum.
Then he loads it up on a wooden ship
And he sends it off on a northern trip

Singing, oh molasses, oh molasses rum
Oh, molasses Old New England tea.
It killed my grandpa, killed my pa.
And it sure as Hell is killing me.
Singing, oh molasses, oh molasses rum.

Susannah could not help but laugh. She decided to stop worrying about what Owen was doing, who this Sherry was, and concluded he had good reason to celebrate. He'd have a sore head tomorrow morning, but otherwise she let her doubts settle, and as it was the night of the winter solstice, she chose to stay peaceful and hopeful.

The remaining group inside was mostly local women, and they were enjoying the decorations and quaintness of the old Dodd house. They seemed quite accustomed to and unbothered by having their men in the barn and didn't particularly miss them.

Many of the women were curious about Susannah, and she found herself fielding questions as they passed around a plate of whoopie pies one of them had made. She mentioned her time in southeast Asia and what she had learned working with an anthropologist. They were curious, so she told the women how she and the professor moved to different locations, and one of the most interesting was in southwestern China. She explained it was one of those minority cultures, the Mosu people, and not only were they ethnically different people from the Chinese, but they were also one of the last remaining matriarchal societies in Asia. This small ethnic group living around China's Lugu Lake in the provinces of Sichuan and Yunnan had remained a matrilineal culture since the thirteenth century, tracing their lineage and subsequent hierarchy through the female side of the family. Susannah and Eric had stayed for one month in a makeshift hostel there. Susannah was mesmerized by the subtle differences in a village community where the women were and always had been the "alpha dogs," so to speak, even to the point where the men were clearly subservient to them in every way. The month they were there was after the harvest, and it was a quiet time of year, so there was more leisure time to be had. She recalled that each day sometime after lunch, the women, who were dressed in bold blue and white colors, would gather to play some intense card and board games in the town square. While the women were engrossed in a public card game, the men watched from the doorways of their homes. Often, they were sweeping the front steps of their little wooden houses but remained out of the public eye.

Susannah explained she was so intrigued by this, watching the women play cards or stand around in discussion with other women while the men hung back. It was clear that if a man walked up to this group, he would do so in a subservient, subdued way. What was strange to her was she saw no resentment in the men's mannerisms, and no ill treatment of them by the women. It was just the way it was. The men were confined to the house, the women were the farmers or merchants or in charge of the business of the day. She experienced many concise, subtle, and tiny differences in the way the men deferred to the women.

Janet had been listening and loved the story. She added, "I think the women out West I met, some of the ranch hands, would absolutely love this kind of society. Some of them are more cowboy than the cowboys."

For curly-haired Marilyn, who worked at the post office in town, she mentioned they all liked how *Downriver with Dodd* was capturing so much of what was unique about their own culture. Rachel, who ran a hair salon out of her home, said all the women enjoyed it and mentioned it when they were getting their hair done.

"It is fun that our town is in the news again," Rachel said. "As far as our society here, I can also say that from what I hear in my salon, it is definitely the women who rule the roost."

Eventually, one of them looked out the window and patted Susannah on the shoulder and said, reassuringly, "Here he is. Owen's coming." Susannah went to the window, too, and watched as he crossed the yard. His strides seemed longer and more powerful than usual as he raced past the schooner to the higher ground where the house sat. He was now at the front door.

"Everyone all right in here?" said a voice as the figure burst into the room. It was Kip, not Owen.

Susannah's face flushed with shame, feeling that Owen was still biding his time in the barn and in no hurry to get to her.

Most of the women in the room had only seen photographs of Kip working in the yard and were impressed that while their men were all still drinking in the barn, a Great Morse Islander had stridden across the icy winter weather to join them.

As he leaned down to kick the snow off his boots, Kip took off his red stocking hat and stood straight up. He towered over everyone. He shook the snow off himself and pressed his hand down to flatten his thick hair. In stretching his arm up, his coat lifted an inch higher, and they could all see the intricately beaded leather belt with its large brass buckle that held up his thick, double-layered work pants. He wiped some light snow off his coat and rubbed his hands together. "Wow. Look at that table!"

They watched as he took strides across the room, with his dark hair flowing, full of body, his style of dress creating some curiosity and intrigue. There were many female eyes on him.

The women made room as he balanced a plate on his knees and sat in an upright chair between the hairdresser and Janet Gregory. He wolfed down his food. Everyone got a chance to talk to him. Although he was a Great Morse Islander, it must have been all those years in New York that had drubbed his accent out of him. He sounded a bit exotic to these women, yet for Susannah, he sounded familiar and spoke the way she did. He didn't pronounce words like eating as "eatin'" or swimming as "swimmin.'" He didn't begin every sentence with a verb like "Got to" or "Getting to."

Eventually, he came over and leaned against the wall in front of Susannah. "The place looks great. I like all the funky decorations and everyone sitting in conversation. It makes me miss New York a bit and reminds me of going to gallery openings and parties."

"I am so used to seeing you in the shipyard," Susannah was enjoying the buzz he had created in the room. "But you do clean up good." They laughed.

"Not so many sea shanties in the art world," he sighed. "But plenty of subjects to paint. Plenty of beauty here to inspire me." He smiled at her.

Until that moment, she had not thought of Kip as an urbanite who could hold his own at a New York City art gallery.

"Do you have your own shows there?" Susannah asked. "Who comes? I would love to see more of your work."

"You would be surprised if I told you who I have met and sold art to," he said. "I already have some sketches of the schooner and the barn but love this antique house, too. I am going to start painting on canvas when I get to Great Morse Island over Christmas."

The word got out that the path from the barn was clear and

suddenly Neville, Quinn, Mysterious Nick, Seb, Sam Dixey, townspeople, and rusticators all poured into the room. They were looking for food. The house guests got up and helped make up plates for them. Finally, Owen, master of the shipyard, stumbled through the front door, making a grand entrance. "Hello! Hi everyone! Got stuck in the barn yappin'!"

Someone said, "Owen, you drunk?"

"I ain't drunk but I been a-drinkin.'" His eyes were sparkling green and a bit wild. He gave Susannah a big smile and walked over to the table and started filling his plate.

The party went on until after midnight when one by one everyone finally left except for Janet, Seb, Kip, and Owen, who had fallen asleep in the only comfortable chair.

The rest of them were sitting in their straight-back chairs lined up against the wall. "I think we need more comfortable furniture in here," Susannah said, feeling a bit embarrassed about the number of chairs lining the walls of the room. "It looks like a funeral parlor."

"It does kind of. But at least the body in that chair is still breathing," Seb said, pointing towards a snoring Owen.

"It's how they had parties in olden times," Kip noted. "They just sat upright like this around a room."

"That is true. All the pictures I have seen of the old days in Ossonet, I never saw a comfortable couch or soft piece of furniture," said Janet.

They spent a peaceful hour just talking to each other, sitting up straight, sharing details of their lives and the people they had met along the way. Everyone was interested in Susannah's travel stories and hearing Kip talk about painting.

"It's kind of amazing you found Ossonet," Janet said to Susannah when she described how she first saw the town. "Most people just drive right past it."

"I almost did!" Susannah said. "I was looking for the historic district, but a lady said there really wasn't one. Still, I was curious to find it."

Seb had been listening. "Well, we are sitting in it," he said.

"Got that right," Janet added, looking at Seb. The two of them smiled at each other. It seemed they did share a feeling of local pride which had taken root among many of the locals on this night.

It was time to go home, and Janet and Seb said goodnight and left together, taking some leftovers with them. Kip had his hat and coat on, swaying a lot.

"Kip, you're a little wobbly," Susannah said. "You should be careful walking over to your boat." There were still some snow squalls and it was hard to see.

"Just got to sit a minute," he said, rubbing his forehead. She grabbed a chair, and he slumped into it, letting out a huge sigh. For a minute she thought he would fall asleep right there. Susannah sat down in the other chair. She then leaned forward to pick up an empty bottle as Kip abruptly sat up and leaned forward to tighten a lace on his boots. Their heads clunked together.

"Ouch," she said, rubbing her head.

"Sorry," he laughed, rubbing his. Perhaps it was the clunk on the head, but he leaned back heavily and suddenly dozed off. She watched him sleep.

She sat next to him in the other chair until she, too, dozed off. Owen, Kip, and Susannah were all asleep in the room.

There was an old ship's clock in the house, and it struck 2 a.m. The ship's bell woke her. Her neck felt sore from sleeping while sitting up straight. She tapped Kip who awoke and abruptly stood up. He was heading to the dooryard, and was about to leave when he noticed something.

"Heh, look at that." He spotted the mistletoe. "It's tradition!" He leaned in and gave her a moist kiss right on the lips.

"Land sakes alive!" he said, using an old Maine expression as he left her standing there in the dooryard. "Happy Solstice!"

CHAPTER TWELVE

It was Christmas Eve, and Susannah was inside the house numbing herself with too many slices of cranberry bread while Owen was alone outside on the schooner, driving huge, heavy metal rods through frames to bolt them down underneath the vessel. Since the crew had taken a break for the holidays, Owen had spent the days leading up to Christmas driving in these long bolts with a heavy sledgehammer. He said the task had to be finished before planking began just after the holidays. The wooden keel that tapered up from the lead to the stem and stern needed drive through bolts that would be tightened with a large nut. The bolt beneath the keel would be exposed to the sea and all it dished out. Owen said that if the keel ever felt in any way loose, these bolts were a way to tighten up the keel and frames throughout its long life. She had been watching him try and shimmy himself beneath the wooden keel with a massive nut to fasten down the keel bolts. He felt she should know that whenever possible, the keel bolts should be tightened. He said it would be a death sentence at sea if a keel became detached from the frames, causing the boat to fill with water and sink. He had begun to tell her a story about a keel that fell off a schooner once at a time when school children were on board and how the captain raced to the dock before the schooner sank to the bottom of the harbor. He was telling her thank God the kids didn't drown, and he had said, "Are you writing this down? For your blog, I mean?"

Susannah had said in an even, resigned tone that "It is Christmastime, and I would rather not write about children almost drowning if we don't continually tighten the keel bolts!"

"Then what will you write about?" he asked rather innocently. She was not sure, but it was Christmas Eve and it wasn't going to be about death by drowning. Not only did it make her sore that he was harping on the subject during what should have been a festive hopeful time of year, but it also occurred to her that he had never acknowledged that she pulled him off the river that night. He could have drowned, and the frightening scene was still fresh in her mind.

He had returned to his work that night after dinner and she spent the evening listening to the metal sledgehammer on metal rods as he drove them through the thick oak . . . Clang! . . .Clang!. . .Clang! There was no banter or sounds of other voices. No warmth or conversation going on between them. Just the Clang! Clang! Clang! She could see he was exhausted, but he showed no signs of stopping.

She went to the window, pacing around the room. She did not want to break his concentration, so she instead wandered back into the kitchen and realized she had already eaten another plate of leftovers, including pie. She stood in the living room and was walking toward the window again when she looked up and noticed the mistletoe.

It was the mistletoe that caused the mishap and the fact that Kip was unsteady on his feet having had a bit too much to drink. That is why the kiss landed on the lips. It was not intentional. Yet, like the whirlpool on the river when the tide changes, on this important night, her feelings about that kiss were deceptively strong.

She had worn herself out waiting for Owen to come in. She went back to the couch and covered herself with a quilt to ward off the draft. She had spent most of this day in a kind of Christmas season coma, watching holiday movies, overeating, feeling sentimental and a little homesick. She lay down on the couch when the noise began again.

"Clang!. . .Clang!. . .Clang!" She covered her ears with a pillow and pulled the quilt over her head. In the distance she could hear the Paul Revere church bells ringing for the Christmas eve candlelight service at the church. The bells were chiming just out of synch with the sound of sledgehammer on metal. *"Between the clanging of the metal and the ringing of the bells,"* went the Edgar Allan Poe poem "The Bells," she thought. She grabbed her computer and looked it up and read the first line:

Hear the sledges with the bells!...Hear the mellow wedding bells...from the rhyming and the chiming of the bells, bells, bells, bells --Bells, bells, bells -- To the moaning and the groaning of the bells.

She made herself laugh as she paced around the house, holding her head in her hands saying, "Bells, bells, bells, the clanging of the bells," as once again another "Clang! Clang! Clang!" came from just outside, and for a moment she could not tell if it was the sledges with the bells she heard or the mellow wedding bells she would not hear this year that made her feel so rattled with the bells, bells, bells.

Susannah started to wonder if this might be the moment she was going to tell Owen about what she really wanted. The fact that she worried about getting older, being thirty-three and feeling holes in her, combined with kissing Kip. . .and reading Poe on Christmas Eve meant she should get a diamond ring. How silly it all sounded.

The stars were out, and Owen had jury-rigged a few industrial lamps so he could see what he was doing. She went to the window thinking Owen might be nearly finished, but he was standing above a frame, lifting the sledgehammer high in the air with the intent of bringing the tool down hard enough to drive the metal stake deep into the keelson. The industrial light cast a long shadow, making him look twice his size. He looked intense. As he lifted the mallet right before bringing it down, his head and his body were like a silhouette against the light on one of the longest nights of the year. She put on her coat and went outside with her long lens camera and took a photograph as he was bringing the sledgehammer around and down hard. Clang! Looking at the photograph through the viewfinder, she could see that with the lamplight against the deep dark sky as a backdrop—with just a few Christmas lights sparkling in the distance—she had captured a very beautiful and singular image. She went back inside and posted it on *Downriver with Dodd.* The image of a man with a sledgehammer with the curved frames all around him set against the dark sky set off a string of comments. Other people must have been home and online, too, that night. Her photo was interpreted by some on the blog as "socialist art," where workers are depicted as larger than life, building a future for the country. Others said that it was a great image of rebirth, and fitting for Christmas. Someone else wrote, "Oh Holy Night. . .what a great photo." What stuck with Susannah when she read the comments was someone called it art. She liked that. She wrote a message to all those who were a part of this great adventure and wished them all the best for a great holiday.

CHAPTER THIRTEEN

As predicted, there was no sparkly ring of engagement for Susannah given by Owen at Christmas. Susannah was not about to say, "I foolishly thought, for all of five minutes, that you might propose to me," so instead told him her low mood was about feeling homesick for her family. She truly was missing home.

To cheer her up, Owen asked her if she wanted to spend a couple of nights away and stay in a hotel. Owen told her he had a great place in mind, and it was just a couple hours' drive north from Ossonet.

She welcomed the idea of a change but then Owen informed her they were going to Great Morse Island. It was because the planking of the schooner was set to begin the first week of January, and they needed all the good oak they could get. Kip, who was home visiting his parents at Great Morse Island, told Owen he could get him some beautifully planed oak planks from Richardsons boatyard, but he would have to haul them back himself.

Owen borrowed Seb's big pickup truck. It was a two-hour drive to the car ferry dock, then an hour across the bay to Great Morse Island. Arriving on the island and driving along toward Richardson's, the snowy landscape resembled an early twentieth century Rockwell Kent painting Susannah had once seen in an art museum. The recent snowfall gave Great Morse Island a beautiful coating of white against the dark, tall evergreens and rolling hills. Just like the painting, the winter sunlight brightened the stark land, which was rugged and sparsely populated, dotted with meadows and tall dark pines leading right up to the water's edge. For nearly 125 years, artists have found inspiration amongst the many islands of coastal Maine and continue to come there to paint. Looking around Great Morse Island, which also had an active artist colony, it seemed that the land and seascapes had not changed that much since the days of Kent, Andrew Wyeth, or George Wesley Bellows. Susannah had read that what kept artists coming to the state was that it had retained a vibrant patchwork of artist colonies, artists-in-residence, and art teachers. Great Morse Island was one of those traditional "colonies," and out of it a young local like Kip had been trained, apprenticed, and had drawn inspiration.

They reached Richardson's and they saw the stovepipe attached to the side of the boat shop and the smoke meant Kip was likely inside. Snowdrifts were piled high against the side of the wooden shingled building, and a pair of cross-country skis and poles were leaning against the heavy wooden door of the shop. There were fresh ski tracks through the snow as if someone had recently gone in. Besides the skis, there were about twenty lobster traps stacked up along with the colored markings of lobster pots showing through the snow. The boat shop was built right on the water's edge with a wooden pier that led out to the harbor. As it was off season, Susannah was amused by a sign that must only be relevant in summer as it said No Diving.

The Richardsons had "expanded" their yard using Quonset hut style buildings much like the ones at the old Gregory yard in Ossonet where the rusticators worked. The main activity, much like the Dodd yard, was in the large barn near the water.

Kip had told them he was building a boat back at Richardson's for a customer, but the project had been delayed, which is why he could manage the time to spend at Dodd's. They were looking forward to seeing it. As they entered the shop, they saw a beautiful wooden yawl under refurbishment supported by marine jack stands with a ladder as the only way to get onto the deck.

Owen climbed up the ladder to the deck just as Kip emerged from the cabin down below. They shook hands.

"By zounds!" Owen said. "You are truly a mar'ster hand, Kip. First-rate finest kind. A fine sailing yacht." The truth was, Owen didn't like custom-built sailing yachts. He felt they were too fancy, from the polished brass winches to the custom-made teak cabin tables and bookshelves. He didn't believe people should just sail recreationally. It should have a purpose to it. Owen didn't have a taste at all for yachtsmen. He was aware that custom-built yachts were the only way to make a living as a boat builder in Maine today. Like Susannah worrying about her newspaper job, Owen was keenly aware now that once the schooner was finished, he did not have any customers knocking on his door for him to build another one. He envied Kip's seeming comfort in this yachting world and knew good workmanship when he saw it. Yet, it wasn't his world.

Kip did look quite relaxed, happy to be home for the holidays. He was wearing dark-rimmed glasses and a gray wool sweater. There was jazz music coming from the portable radio down below in the cabin. Although when Kip was hard at work in Ossonet, he was impressively fast, agile, strong, and rugged, here he looked like a sophisticated artisan, a "yachtie," or fine art painter sipping coffee and listening to jazz. Susannah was intrigued that he could straddle these different worlds.

As they stood on deck, Susannah asked about the differences between the more rugged double-sawn frame schooner at the Dodd yard and this custom-made wooden sailing yacht. Kip explained a big difference is the yacht has a cockpit. Schooners are open with plenty of room to walk around and were built with massive holds to carry fish. The design had not changed that much, although there were cabin tops covering the hold. But there were at best benches to sit on or the deck itself. There was no seating plan, and the helmsman was obliged to stand up and steer the entire time. A cockpit enabled everyone to sit together, socially, and the social aspect of sailing for pleasure was one of the biggest differences between a pleasure craft and a work boat.

"So, you want to come on down below and have a look before we get the planks?"

The cabin's interior had many coats of varnish, giving it a deep chestnut brown glow. The joinery work was beautifully put together. There were little touches all around the cabin—a navigational station beautifully varnished and a lovely, large mahogany table for meals.

Susannah walked to the forward cabin at the front end of the boat. There was a comfortable forward room which could sleep two, a closet for clothes, a marine bathroom or "head," and hand-built bookcases on both sides of the cabin above the bed. The interior wood featured inlaid hardwood ornamentations that resembled the designs of

Kip's betel handle. Kip had done all the intricate woodwork.

Susannah sat next to Owen at the fine wood table. Nearby, Kip was leaning against the galley stove. He had put the tea kettle on.

"Great work if you can get it, Kip," Owen said with a twinge of envy.

"Only way to survive around here," Kip said as he poured them some tea. "I wish we did have more schooner customers, but mostly we build and maintain these for yachtsmen."

"I wish they liked to sail schooners," Owen said, sounding a bit deflated.

"They would if they could!" Kip said. "Most sailors don't know what they are missing. I wish we could build schooners here too."

"Tell me about it," Owen scoffed. "We could get them the best money can buy."

As she listened to Kip and Owen talk, she envied them both for their shipwright skills and devotion to it and how they had both been mentored by others to learn this unique trade. Like Neville Joseph who had his elders on St. Vincent, they had all been given a great opportunity to learn. There were very few, if any, girls who would have learned through apprenticeships or hanging around boatyards in those days. Realistically, a grown man might not have been willing to teach a thirteen- or fourteen-year-old girl; it would seem unnatural. In fact, Janet had told her that when she was growing up, girls were not allowed to hang around the boatyards. It was off limits "for a reason" they were told.

As she watched Kip and Owen talk, she wanted to be included in the conversation, yet she did not share that experience, passion, or background. She had been documenting the schooner build for months and had gained some expertise, yet it seemed she needed another thirty years before she could be considered knowledgeable.

It was time to get the planks they needed. They would meet Kip later at his parents' house for a small New Year's Eve party.

Susannah and Owen were now ready to get to the inn for their long awaited "hotel sex" that Owen kept talking about during the drive and the ferry crossing.

"How did you learn, how did someone like Kip learn?" she asked as she distractedly lay down on the bed, not really in the mood.

He slowly undressed and marveled at the big puffy pillows on the bed. "Oh, nice down pillows!" he exclaimed as he turned the covers over. "Sheets!" he said as if he had never seen them before. He then walked over to the window. It had a view of the water. He grabbed the large curtain to the room and yanked it hard, so the room was dark.

"To be shipwrights. To work with tools, I mean," Susannah pressed on. Owen stood in front of her completely naked, and she had to laugh as he was still wearing a hat. He jumped into bed.

"We stood around and watched the older guys do it," he said, getting comfortable. "I spent every day after school with the old timers and rusticators, watching them work."

"I don't think that would happen with a girl," Susannah insisted. "I doubt Janet Gregory spent that much time in a shipyard."

"I don't know." Owen was distracted. "I always figured she wasn't interested."

He pulled up the covers. He snuggled up against her, although she was still lying above her covers.

"Why, do you want to stand around and watch us work?" he asked her, and tried to get her to hunker down with him, to take off her top and pants and get into position. "It is the only way to learn."

"Yeah, but. . . just standing around?" Susannah said.

"See, with wooden shipbuilding, you learn the hard way, but you can't get pushed out of the profession because there is no profession anymore."

"I suppose you are right!" she agreed. "It is like working for a newspaper. I suppose you are in an industry that is already dead, and my industry is in its dying phase. I see a bright future for us both."

"Maybe the difference is I have passion for my work," Owen ventured, as he stroked her hair and pulled gently at her top, trying to get her to pull it up over her head.

"Ouch." Susannah hated that he saw it so simply.

"I think you have to find something you are passionate about," Owen said, trying to be nice. "What is it you really want? I mean it doesn't seem like you enjoy newspaper work, and they keep giving the good assignments to the other guy."

"I have passion for a lot of things," she said in her defense, although maybe he was partly right. "I know I want to be in a relationship with you. I realize that may not be what you mean."

"I guess what I mean is people, I mean people like you who have not found something by now, may not have that same passion, deep down, in your soul," Owen ventured.

"Like in my soul?" Susannah asked. To think she had been hoping for an engagement ring from someone who thought she had no soul.

Owen nodded yes, realizing he hit on something uncomfortable to talk about.

"You mean, you are saying I have no soul." Susannah knew that he didn't exactly mean that. "I don't put body and soul into anything?"

"You have been putting a lot of your body and soul into me," Owen explained. "But what about you? What are you going to do?"

"I don't know." She was confused. "What are you going to do? You can't spend your whole life in the barn calling yourself the 'historic district' of Ossonet."

"Hence, the schooner I am building in my front yard," he shot back.

"I see," she said. She remained defensive while he was also teasing her with foreplay. She resisted as she was now about to make love to someone who did not think she had a soul. She also hated that he did surely have a point. He was no longer idling in the barn. He was a man with a mission. She had thought maybe it was her mission, too, but now she was not sure.

"I traveled all over the world in my twenties, Owen," she argued. "I saw people and places that may no longer exist in ten years. I worked like an anthropological student. I filled journals with it, I loved it. Then I came home. End of story."

"You had passion for what you were doing then," he said.

She felt like she had to stand up for something. But he was right. Since returning from her life overseas, she had lost that dream, and although she was living in a shipyard with a schooner in frame, she had been simply standing at the window observing it all. At least she could change this.

"Owen, can I work with you when you begin planking this coming week? I will do my newspaper job at night."

"Sure, I guess." He didn't really think she would follow through.

"I really need to try at least," she said.

"Fine, can we have our hotel sex now?"

She finally undressed and got under the covers. It felt good to be warm, and she pressed herself against him. He stroked her legs and hips and rubbed her breasts. She pressed her mouth on his dry lips and tousled the top of his head. She noticed that his hair was getting thinner, and he had been outside so long most of his skin was dry and rough. She did not feel aroused, and he sensed her hesitation towards him.

"What can I do to get you in the mood?" his green eyes sparkling as he asked her.

She answered directly. "How about an engagement ring?" she half joked.

"Is that what you are really passionate about?" he asked her. She had to admit that she wasn't sure, so she gave it a shot.

"They say that passion is temporary, but love is permanent," she said.

"Come on, honey," Owen said. "Just lay quiet. Relax." They were burrowed in bed together on the last day of the year, and the new year was full of promise, not regrets, but no 'I will always love you' either. She rallied herself and rolled onto her back. He took each of her arms and placed them over her head and pressed his hands on each and gave them a little pressure, as if to keep them in place. She reached for him and held his cock—caressed it and cupped her hand around it. She was wet and ready for him, and he was hard; both got lost in the sexual act with her wanting him inside her, him feeling himself about to come.

Afterwards, she wanted to talk some more but held back. He wanted to make love again and not talk. Expressing his feelings was not comfortable territory for Owen, and she had already said too much. Better just to talk about the boat—an object of Owen's complete affection.

They arrived late at Kip's parents' home, and it was just a couple hours away from ringing in the New Year. They enjoyed meeting Kip's mother, Nita. Nita was one half Micmac but had married an old Yankee of Scottish descent whom she met while getting their master's degrees in art and teaching. Both his parents pursued college teaching careers, but Nita had remained devoted to Micmac cultural artifacts and North American tribal art. Nita had cultivated a real love for Inuit soapstone sculptures, and she had often been to coastal settlements of Labrador, meeting Inuit artists. Because Nita made pilgrimages to these remote places, she helped support the artists by setting up a small gallery on

Great Morse Island where she sold their work.

Kip also had long ago learned to carve with soapstone. Sculpting was one of his passions, but he also produced oil and watercolor landscapes and abstract paintings. It was like being with a museum guide as Nita was explaining to them that the composition, use of light, and the open spaces of the pieces Kip used seemed to convey a longing, searching message. She explained that his paintings had a mystical quality that was very intriguing to art buyers.

Kip saw his mother giving a tour and said, "Mom, *Giju*, are you making up stories about me again?"

Giju, the Micmac name for mother, still translated into her boasting a little about her son to his friends. She finished with, "Kip has done well in New York, and I think it is because of his color choices and the starkness of the landscape. There is a lot of longing for open spaces I see in it. Maybe that is what New Yorkers feel too."

As it was closing in on the New Year, Kip tried to steer Owen and Susannah away from his *giju* so the friends could all celebrate together. As he led them away, Kip gave Nita a quick kiss. "Thank you, Mom. Happy New Year."

It was getting close to midnight. Owen and Kip toasted glasses.

"Happy New Year, Kip! Thanks for everything this year, man! I am sorry that I never loved you, really. Otherwise, you have been great." And he patted Kip on the back. Kip then gave him a big bear hug and said, "I never loved you either, Owen. Happy New Year, man. I can't wait to see how the schooner looks when we get the planks on her."

Just then a woman named Claire MacInnis came up to them all and said hello. Neville, Mysterious Nick, and Kip had all told Susannah about Claire. She ran the MacInnis shipyard on the mainland which was passed down through her family. She was set to expand to high-end custom yacht building trade, which was where all the work was today. To Susannah's surprise, Claire read *Downriver with Dodd*.

"You do a great job on that!" Claire said, complimenting Susannah. "I am so intrigued by it all. Is Owen Dodd here?"

"Yeah, that's him." He was standing right next to her. "It is so great to meet a woman shipyard owner, wow!"

"You should come up and see us," Claire said.

Although it was a few minutes to spare before midnight, Claire asked if it was okay to talk to the "one and only" Owen Dodd. Susannah said, "Go for it," as she felt it would be good for Owen to talk to someone running a growing, successful shipyard.

Owen was talking to Claire MacInnis and was busy shaking hands with others from Great Morse Island when the clock struck midnight.

"Thank you for everything, Kip. Happy New Year!" she fumbled. He had something in his hand.

"What is that?" she asked.

It was an Inuit-style sculpture of black soapstone made in the shape of an owl.

"That is beautiful, Kip!" She rubbed it as if it were Aladdin's lamp. She loved the feel of the soapstone and the look of the owl. The carving felt like a friend.

He told her that the Inuit see the owl as a personal totem. Or a spirit animal that they are connected to. The owl is the most "symbolic of a life transition or change."

"It's like a talisman, good luck for the New Year and being safe on the river. "*Pasu'l Pana'ne!*" he said in Micmac. "Happy New Year."

Owen had a small crowd around him, and they were all heading into the other room to find a place to sit down. Kip was standing there in front of her, seconds into a new year. They kissed as was tradition.

CHAPTER FOURTEEN

The first full week of January came in bitter cold, and the river basin surrounding the Dodd shipyard froze up. What had been whitecaps or froth on the river in the fall became stacks of ice sheets that grew thicker and more hazardous as winter tightened its grip.

On this first day back to work, the bright sun reflecting on the snow made it feel like a fresh new beginning. It was not only the start of a new year, but it marked the first day of planking the schooner, a sight that had not been seen here since the middle of the last century.

Kip and Owen had moved Kip's boat to an area of the river that tended not to freeze up, so he had a slightly longer walk to the Dodd shipyard. As Kip walked along the road, wearing his heavy work gloves, a pair of tan insulated Carhartt pants as well as his beaded jacket and red stocking cap, the few cars that passed him on the road tooted at him and waved. He was pleased by the greetings, and he waved back to the unfamiliar faces in the passing cars. He wondered if people recognized him because of the photos in *Downriver with Dodd*. He made a stop in the store to buy a coffee, and to his surprise bumped into Janet Gregory, who was in the store with her father.

"Happy New Year, Kip," Janet said, giving him a warm greeting and a quick hug.

"Happy New Year, Janet," Kip replied. He also shook hands with her father, who looked quite dapper in his winter coat, wool cap, scarf, tweed jacket, and tie. "Happy New Year, Mr. Gregory."

"Happy New Year, young Kip," he said as he held himself with his walker and shook hands. "You can call me O.G."

Kip shared the news with O.G. and Janet that the steam box was getting stoked up and planking of the schooner would begin.

"Got to have many hands to bend that wood on while it's hot," O.G. said. "Otherwise, it'll fight you every step of the way. Got enough men?"

Kip nodded yes. "And we got a woman too."

"Land sakes alive. Say what?" said O.G. cupping his hand to his ear.

Janet blurted, "What? Who?"

Kip smiled. "Susannah's starting today."

Janet repeated the news to her father, but she, too, was a bit taken aback.

"Well, isn't that the cat's foot," O.G. said with slight disapproval in his tone. "You took the gimp all out of me."

They respectfully waited to see what else he might say. The old master paused and then said, "Got to pay attention to the curves of the ship when bending on a plank, not the female ones. That ship's going to look mighty lopsided, mind you!"

Janet almost spilled her coffee when she turned to her father. "Oh, come on, Dad!"

"That's okay, Mr. Gregory. I welcome the distraction." He smiled at Janet but all he got from her was a raised eyebrow. At that moment, Sherry Goodwin walked into the store. She had recently moved back to town and was working in Clydebank. She wore a heavy dose of perfume that permeated the store. Like most locals, she went straight to the warming pots of coffee and poured herself some as she listened in on the town talk. Joining the conversation uninvited was a common thing to do in the small space of their local town store. Sherry was no exception. She'd clearly been listening and now turned toward them all and said, "Owen used to tell me that women in a shipyard brought bad luck."

"No, the old saying is that women on ships bring bad luck," Janet corrected her. "But God knows, sometimes the old seed folks passed down these stories. I can't imagine an old-timer passing that superstition along," and she rolled her eyes in the direction of her own father.

Mr. Gregory nodded in agreement with Sherry. "We had so many men looking for work back then, we didn't have to hire women."

"Owen always stopped me from going to the old shipyards when we were in high school," Sherry rattled on. "We would hang out all day, but once we got near the old Gregory or Dodd shipyards, he would hold up his hand like a cop and say STOP." Sherry shrugged. "I usually went home thinking I was bad luck."

"I see now how he was carryin' sail," Janet said, knowing Owen well enough to see he had drawn an imaginary line with Sherry so he could join the men and tinker with tools and learn from the rusticators to his heart's content.

"Owen is quicker'n chain lightning and smart enough to do anything, but he is a damn fool to have a woman in the shipyard!" O.G. insisted, still chewing on Kip's news.

"Not speaking for Owen," Kip said, and then looked respectfully at Mr. Gregory, "because I just tend to my own knittin', but we'll need help in the spring when it's time to paint and putty her."

Kip was now in a hurry, as he could see smoke belching in the distance in the shipyard. Owen had built the steam box over the holidays, and it was the epitome of Yankee ingenuity. The box resembled a very long pine coffin, but it had a little door on one end that opened and shut. Steam from a vat of boiling water was pumping into this coffin-like box so when the small door opened, steam heat would pour out. This meant it was time to slide a plank into the box and close the door. To achieve this, Owen had jury-rigged an old oil burner barrel and was feeding that with wood and coal and stoking the fire. This heated up an enclosed one-hundred-gallon kettle settled just above the fire. A rubber tube connected to the kettle piped steam into the box. The steam heat and humidity served to soften the stiff boards of oak. They would come out of the box flexible and springy, which meant the workers could bend and clamp them in place on the schooner before they cooled.

Kip knew the smoke meant Owen was firing up the steam box, and he excused himself. He had to get to the yard. Kip tipped his hat to them, and all his thick, wavy hair tumbled down, as it so often did. He quickly ran his hand through his hair to pull it out of his handsome face and put his hat back on as he left.

Janet Gregory was initially taken aback that Susannah Pierce, a woman from Philadelphia, would now become the first female to ever work in an Ossonet shipyard. She was disappointed that honor wouldn't be hers but knew this was not Susannah's fault.

For Janet, the sentiments of "the old seed folks"—as Mainers called their ancestors—were ingrained in her. Born more than thirty years after the last shipyard closed, there had been no working yard for her when growing up, yet she knew a great deal about shipyard life from her parents and grandparents. Besides, back then the Gregory and Dodd properties still had old-timers and kids like Owen there all the time. It had always been an unspoken rule that it was off limits to women and girls, because of the "itinerants" and "drifters" who were "always on the hind end of nothing," the locals said. These itinerants turned out to be today's rusticators, and not only were they harmless, but they had also passed down all they knew to young men like Owen. And yet, all her life, Janet was duly warned, especially when she was "ripe enough to rattle," that the shipyard was no place for a female. And, like Sherry, Janet had also abided by that same imaginary line most of her life.

Janet was also told, time and time again, that when shipbuilding had ended in the late 1940s, it was out of Ossonet's hands, and that the town had had no part of the decisions that had allowed it to happen. Yet during WWII, when so many men left jobs to go to war and women filled in for them across the country, the town's stubborn refusal to let the town women work in the shipyards had ultimately been part of the reason why the boatbuilding industry completely collapsed. Not enough men came back soon enough at war's end to diversify and keep the craft going, as other Maine towns and cities continued to build, like Claire MacInnis's family or the Richardsons. They built everything and anything. Lobster boats, fishing vessels, and many converted to fiberglass and cold molded wood and Coast Guard vessels and sailing yachts. Ossonet's calcified, shrunken industry— where they built the most famous and most enduring wooden ships in America—died out in part because of a stubborn old superstition.

As she stood there, looking at her ailing father, Janet felt the burden of her own family's lack of vision. She realized, too, that on her first day working in the shipyard, Susannah might need some moral support.

"Come on, Dad, hurry up. Let's go down to the yard before we miss that first plank."

For the first time ever, Janet was rushing her father to get down to the yard instead of the other way around.

"I want to see this," she said, smiling to herself at the idea of her friend Susannah sticking a finger in the eye of the old Ossonet forbears.

Susannah was in the house dressing for her first day as a shipwright apprentice. To get ready for her new job, she had scoured Clydebank, searching for the kind of work clothes she needed, but there was nothing among women's clothing. So, she went to the marine supply store and bought a thick pair of men's flannel-lined Carhartt overalls, plus a big, padded denim work jacket, thick socks, and a pair of steel-toed work boots.

As she now dressed to go out, she was not only struggling with the weight of it all, but she was a bit embarrassed by the stiffness of her new clothes. She felt unwieldy. To add to her bulk, she was wearing a fur-lined sheepskin Mongolian nomad's hat that had a decorative, pointy top. As she was heading for the door, her thick frame nearly knocked over a chair. She caught a glimpse of herself in a mirror and had to laugh. The layered clothing and Mongolian hat had her thinking for a moment she was a Sumo wrestler. Oh, but she loved her hat! Five years prior, she and Eric had gotten a special one-month visa to visit some of the last nomadic people living in Mongolia. She had bonded with one family, and they had given her this handcrafted piece for winter protection from the eastern Mongolian steppes.

As she huffed and puffed her way through the dooryard and out into the bitter cold, marking the first time that a woman had ever worked or apprenticed in an Ossonet yard, Janet tooted the horn of her car and could not suppress a laugh. They waved to each other. Neville, Seb, Mysterious Nick, and the rusticators looked a bit surprised and amused. Owen had told them nothing and now gave them no explanation as to why she was there. He had not realized she was serious about all of this when they were away and had no work plan for her. So, they were waiting on Owen to fill them in.

All Owen said was, "Got the coffee ready?"

Taken aback, Susannah was sure that Owen was going to explain to them that she was now working with them. He did not. So, she returned with a full coffee pot, balancing some mugs, milk, and sugar in her arms. She wondered if this was a kind of test Owen was giving her.

Owen said, "You can put it right on top of the box. Perfect, that'll keep it hot," he said as she placed the coffee pot and mugs on top of the steam box.

"See," he said, and was very pleased as he touched the warm top of the box. "It won't always be this slow going, but we can drink our coffee while we wait for the first planks to steam."

Owen was keen to get going and was stuffing more scrap wood and coal in to feed the already roaring fire when Kip arrived.

"Making moonshine?" Kip asked as the whole setup somehow looked like a backwoods distillery.

"Did you take the oil burner out of your own house, mon?" Neville asked as Owen stoked the coals and got the fire really going after adding the wood.

"Seb got it from God knows where, and last week he helped me attach this hose to the box," Owen said.

Mysterious Nick added, "Good job on the steam box door, Owen. Finest kind."

Owen said, "Had time while you guys were away. Couldn't stop thinking about all of you, though, God, I missed you all!" he joked.

"Not me," Mysterious Nick affirmed, and the others nodded in agreement.

"Nope. Not feeling it," another one said.

"Well, I never really loved any of you anyway." Owen smiled as he opened the door of the empty steam box a crack. Steam poured out.

Eager to get started, the men went to the drying shed and loaded two planks in and shut the door.

"Phew. Now I know what to do when I need to blow off steam," Seb said, a bit winded.

"God, I love you, Seb," Owen muttered.

As Owen, Kip, Seb, Neville, Mysterious Nick, and other rusticators all leaned in around the warm steam box as the wood cooked, they inadvertently left no room for Susannah to squeeze in.

As Susannah found a place near the warmth of the steam box, she felt like that new kid on the first day of school, not knowing exactly what to do and realizing they had already started and could easily continue working without her.

"Looks like a mar'ster hand has joined us," Neville ventured to Susannah, trying to be encouraging by comparing her to a master shipwright.

"Finest kind," Seb added, looking slightly less convinced.

"Thanks for the coffee, Susannah," Mysterious Nick said.

Kip tipped his hat to her, trying to show his approval.

Like chefs baking bread, they waited to pull out hot, freshly baked planks from the oven. They timed the planks at about thirty minutes in the box as the texture of the wood is key to be able to press or bend it with force before it cools down enough for the wood to splinter or snap.

It was time. They opened the door. "Okay! Positions everyone!" Owen yelled. The men scattered across the yard to their appointed positions as if they were setting up for a game play. "Plank is near about ready," Owen called out. "Ready down there?" Neville and Susannah stood ready by the oven while the others were already at the schooner. They had to carry it about twenty yards.

As soon as the steam box opened, with a specific destination for each piece in his mind, Owen called out, "Starboard aft first plank coming out!" Wearing gloves that resembled oven mitts, they pulled the first long, hot plank out of the box. The plank let off steam in the cold morning air. Susannah did not understand where the hell the plank was supposed to go. She tried to grab a piece of it, too, to help, but she had thin gloves on, making it too hot and too hard for her to grip. Neville held on to the bulk of the plank, but he made room for her to grab the tail end. As they moved quickly across the snowy yard, the steam burn hurt but she held on. "Keep moving!" Owen shouted, and he had now rushed down to the schooner, waiting for the first plank.

Neville reached them with Susannah barely holding on. Seb, Kip, and Owen took the plank, and using their shoulders, backs, and hands to wrestle the wood around the designated frames, they bent the wood as far as it would flex. They fastened heavy clamps between the frame and the plank and turned them tight. The goal was to keep its curved line intact and prevent the plank from springing back to its natural straightness. Susannah stood watching, amazed at how the wood was soft enough to bend. It reminded her of the soft, pliable baguettes the baker takes out of the oven which become stale and as stiff as a bat only a day later.

They started at the bottom of the vessel, just above the keel, and went up bit by bit. For the first plank, they were all crouched under the frames, kneeling in the snow and ice.

"Heh, Kip, hand me that clamp," said Seb. "Might as well get it bent on as tight as we can." As Kip handed the clamp to Seb, Owen crouched low too, examining the wood up close.

"This is a beauty. I'm sure this oak came from around here," Owen said.

"I don't know, Owen," Kip said. "Looks to me like nice white oak from nearer to the County." Although there are sixteen counties in Maine, Kip was referring to Aroostook County on the Canada-Maine border. Mainers always referred to this wilderness area as the County. White oak was more plentiful there and coveted for shipbuilding.

"No, it's local. I had to pull a few nails out of it when I was sanding it," Owen said.

Each plank needed at least twenty clamps to hold it tight. Once the plank was clamped on, one of them took a power drill and drilled carefully placed holes through the soft wood that reached deep into the frame. This enabled them to secure the plank to the frame by driving both wooden tree-like nails, or trunnels, with their heavy wooden betels as well as bronze screws. The wooden betels were essential in that the wooden mallet offered a lot less stress on the plank than if they smashed the sides of the plank with a blunt metal sledgehammer. The idea was not to pulverize the wood but simply drive the trunnels deep into the frame. Setting the trunnels right, the rounded peg went into the round hole while the square trunnel ends served as the nail head. By turning the trunnel around, it would be like trying to drive a square peg into a round hole, which was impossible. Once the trunnels went in, the square pegs remained and covered the plank, looking like large clothespins. Soon enough, they would be sawed off and land in a pile beneath the schooner, and what remained would be a smooth hull with holes filled. The wooden nails were not quite enough insurance that the hull would stay together, so they also used expensive bronze screws to anchor the planks to the frame. The screws were driven so deep into the plank and frame that they left an empty shaft hole near the plank surface. To prevent water seeping in, these holes were capped off with a small bung—a rounded piece of wood that was the exact shape of a gumdrop—that plugged up the "bunghole."

While they were getting the plank bent around the frame, a second steaming plank was about ready. More people had heard about the planking and had come by to watch or help. Eager Quinn was ready at the steam box, but he had forgotten his gloves. Susannah loaned him hers as she had been instructed by Owen to start cutting small bungholes to plug into the planks after the bronze screw went in. They worked this way the first day, and by late afternoon there were a lot of men gathered around the steam box, watching, helping, staying warm and enjoying the sight. Kip, Owen, Mysterious Nick, and Neville had muscled the planks much of the day. Susannah was bringing freshly cut bungholes to some of the rusticators, who were plugging up the places that had bronze nails drilled through.

Susannah had stuck with it, although it was time for her to get started on her newspaper work, so she carried the last "bucket of bungs"—as everyone called them—over to the schooner. Like a ski hill, the area around the schooner had lost its snowpack and was very slippery after so many people had walked over it throughout the day. As she nearly reached the schooner, she slipped, and her bucket of freshly cut bungs went flying everywhere. She landed hard on her back, and the impact made her hat fall off. She was worried about losing all the bungs, so she started crawling around on the slippery snowpack trying to gather them back up. It was too late when she noticed her hat had somehow slid and been blown down toward the river and was now on the outside edge of a frozen block of ice. She raced down and tried to grab it as it was blown farther away. It had slipped out of reach, so she stepped onto the slab of ice and leaned towards it when suddenly Owen yelled, "Don't go near there!" She was shocked to hear him yell at her as he had pretty much ignored her all day. "Stop! Susannah, get off!"

Susannah stopped in her tracks. She was so close to getting the hat, but she obeyed him and dashed off the river for higher ground just as a deep ripple from the still flowing water beneath the frozen blocks of ice made a strange, groaning sound. The ice floe moved, and her hat slid through two slabs and disappeared into the water. She watched with horror as she lost it forever. That beautiful Mongolian hat!

She knew it was silly to grieve an object, but she was very shaken. The hat was never meant to be used in a Maine shipyard but by nomadic people living in yurts on an open plain. Standing there on the river's edge, exposed to the cold wind without her cherished hat, she felt a fool to ever think she could belong in either place.

Owen walked over to her and looked concerned. "It's not like pond ice," he told her. "It can grab you like a bear trap and pull you under." She later learned that a local boy had disappeared this way when Owen's father was young. Ever since, every child had been warned and was rightfully petrified of the killer ice.

"My hat. I loved that hat. I almost had it."

Owen put his arm around her and felt a twinge of guilt. She could have gone under the ice and drowned just then. He resolved to try and be nicer, although he still could not quite understand why she insisted so much on being there. Like many generations of Ossonet men, he did not really see a place for a woman in the shipyard, and this incident confirmed it.

CHAPTER FIFTEEN

Carrying heavy, hot planks from the steam box to the schooner was made more difficult with each fresh dump of new snow. The crew was too busy to shovel snow with each new storm, so they simply trudged through the powder carrying the planks. Eventually, they forged a packed-down path, good until the next snowstorm. They would all inch along toward the schooner, never to veer off or end up with one leg stuck in deep snow.

As they trudged along, Susannah would stumble along to keep up while holding the plank. At times, she might grab Neville or inadvertently latch onto Mysterious Nick by the coat to steady herself. There was confusion on which direction to carry the plank as they got closer to the schooner. In unison, they could all lose their balance and slip while steering the unwieldy hot wood in a new direction based on Owen's command. He and Kip were often waiting at the ship to "bend it on" with large clamps and betels. Everyone was in a hurry to get the wood curved and in place before it cooled and became rigid. The men had a certain agility carrying the planks with their strong arms and torsos, while Susannah tried to make up for her lack of upper body strength through stamina and determination.

By mid-winter they had made a lot of progress, and the planking had moved up toward the middle of the hull towards midships. It kept snowing, but the accumulating inches now became a useful work platform. The snow platform rose almost in tandem with the planking so they could bend planks on at midships without the need for any scaffolding to reach it.

Although Owen had gradually come to accept his new routine with Susannah, he was keenly aware that she wasn't skilled like the others. He noticed she had been fumbling and stumbling, and he knew it would not be long now before the snow would melt and they would need to climb higher with the planks. This would mean she would be carrying planks up wobbly scaffolding—at least one story above ground.

Owen spoke to her, and only her, repeatedly on the dangers of getting up there with the planks, and that shook her confidence. When alone at night, much of the conversation centered on Owen's hopes that he would not run out of wood, that there would be no accidents, and he reminded her of his to do list as his mind raced. Susannah found herself, occasionally, answering him with a "Yes, boss" or "No, boss," but as his doubts grew about her skills, she became agitated, as he seemed to want her off the job more than on it. Early each morning before the others arrived, she sat there, head down, drinking coffee and worrying with him and worrying about them. Trying to address the heightened tension between them were always conversations interrupted by the arrival of the men. The sound of someone kicking snow off their boots or clearing their throat outside saw Owen jump up as it was time to fire up the steam box.

When they had a few minutes alone at night, she would show him the most recent copy of the Clydebank News, pointing out her byline. He would sit down then and flip through it quickly and compliment her work. If she wasn't in the room, he would then crumple it up and use the newspaper to start fires in the steam box and the woodstove and then get back to work.

Because the wood stove was the main source of heat it was always plenty warm inside by midday. Susannah started to think of this as a thawing out time, because as the men came in for lunch each day, the shipwrights' clothes were frozen and wet from hours outside in below-freezing temperatures or yet another snowstorm. They all wore the same thickly lined Carhartt overalls and barn coats, and by midday their clothes were iced over. If they were wet through, the men stripped down to just their long underwear. They would pull off their overalls and drape them near the woodstove to dry out. Boots, socks, and sometimes shirts also needed to dry. Susannah tried to appear indifferent as they undressed. The men's physiques were on display as they wandered half-dressed around the room trying to thaw out. With so much wet clothing, the kitchen and dining area steamed up with evaporating ice, snow, and sweat. As they gathered around the table for hot drinks and meals, she was often squeezed in next to Neville and Kip and found herself getting warm because of their body heat. She bobbed between them, arms and legs touching almost naturally. Perhaps this is why Janet Gregory's grandmother had been told not to feed the men or let them in her house, not to mention working side by side with them. With all the clothes coming off, the men's bodies thawing all around her, and the warm banter, this might have caused Owen a twinge of jealousy. It apparently did not.

"Plank forty-two goes on next. The forward broad strake right plank, to be specific. Got to get that into the steam box after lunch."

At lunch one day, Kip said, "Heh, do any of you mind if I mention something? The sheer lines of the hull don't seem to line up quite right. It looks a little rough."

As this was the first schooner they had ever built, everyone had begun to wonder if Owen was simply eyeballing it. That was the old way it was done, they figured. Owen was not taking daily measurement of the curvature, and he was so focused on the planking that he had not noticed that the boat was looking boxy.

"What about some red yarn and white chalk to make sure the dimensions are true. Learned it when I was an apprentice at Richardson's," Kip suggested. "It is the easiest way to keep an eye on the curve."

"Got to look at the breadth of it more," Owen agreed.

"Right," Kip said.

As they all got up from the table to head back to the afternoon's work, Owen said, "It's all about the curves with you, Kip!" And jabbed him with his elbow. Susannah felt a twinge, thinking that Owen was making a double entendre and was jealous of her flirtation with Kip. He was not. The debate seemed to be exclusively about curves on the ship and was ongoing between Owen and Kip.

Owen was going to rely on a dubbing axe and power sanders to grind the vessel into shape, but Kip, the fine artist, saw it differently. He insisted on looking at its shape each time they put on a plank. As it came together, he would stand back and look at it as if he were holding a palette and paintbrush. He wanted the aesthetics to show a finely crafted hull from the beginning, while Owen, who was impatient, just wanted to get it done the Ossonet way and just make sure the hull was tighter than the bark on a tree. There was a conflict brewing between art and functionality, and the two men stood firm in their beliefs.

"Maybe I can point out to you what I mean," Kip said, instead of trying to make Owen see his points. "Take this string, chalk, and battens. Walk it down the hull and look. You need to memorize its curves, shape, and dimensions."

They would stand at the front end of the boat, looking very small compared to its growing height, width, and length overall.

"Good eye, Mon," Neville would chime in as he was very much in agreement with Kip. "Good to remember that this man Kip has an eye for a yacht."

"This is not a yacht!" Owen said firmly. Still, he knew that Kip's insistence on keeping an eye on the shape was going to enhance its beauty. They all started to pick up Neville's description of "tending to the sweet lines," and it took more time and patience than Owen could manage.

Owen saw the larger work in front of him, but Kip could visualize the shape and lines and how to achieve a smoother, beautifully sanded, or "fared" hull once they began that phase of it. Susannah thought she had uncovered an interesting story of two different perspectives on the same work, so she wrote a blog post about it. Without realizing it, she had elevated Kip's skills to Owen's level in the eyes of her readers. Kip was also spending time in the barn building the rudder, which was like a large puzzle piece. It would be installed as soon as the planks were above midships, and he was not only putting it together with some masterful joinery work, but he also had that eye for shape and beauty. Owen privately thought it was too pretty. Kip was being depicted more often as the artist, and the photos of his work illustrated it too. When he wasn't working, he was painting the shipyard scene, and she photographed him at his easel. It was a hit with readers, and he had asked if he could hang some of the finished work around the barn. Sometimes people came by to see the schooner, while others came by to see what Kip had painted. He captured the dramatic flair of their wardrobes set against the harsh winter setting and the progression of the schooner. The scene had also inspired some talented photographers to come down each day and shoot. They would send their photographs to Susannah, and she would post them on social media along with photos of Kip's paintings. Corncob or traditional pipe smoking had always been a habit of wooden shipwrights, and it seemed these men were a bit addicted to the puff-puff on the pipe while they worked outside through the day. The readers could not get enough of the photos and stories of the handsome West Indian in a Cossack hat smoking a pipe, or the artist, Kip, with his red fur-trapper hat, his corncob pipe, colorful betel mallet with its carved handle, or his paints, easel, and palette. Or Owen, with his dark blue oiled cap, his wire-rimmed glasses, and his colorful wool sweaters, all covered with wood shavings.

The month of March, as Mainers say, comes in like a lion and goes out like a lamb, and as it gradually got warmer, people around the county would come by to watch them bend a plank on a frame. Folks enjoyed seeing each other and getting together and watching the hull really take shape. They sometimes shouted out comments and observations, and banter started between the shipwrights and the townspeople from across the way.

"Some busy, Owen?" they asked, knowing that he was very busy.

Owen would say back, "Wicked busy!"

"I know it," they would say.

The shipwrights would continue working unless Owen spotted someone in the crowd whom he hadn't seen for some time.

"Whaddya been up to all wintah?" he shouted at an old friend, dropping all his r's, as Mainers often do.

"Out in the willywags," the answer would come back. "Uptah camp. Ice fishing," referring to the lakes region where he had a small cabin.

One day one of the observers shouted out, "Got a date for launching her?"

"Hahd sayin,' not knowin'!" Owen said in a thicker than usual Maine accent.

"Yessah," they said, nodding. "Ayuh," they said in agreement.

"Rudders goin' in next!" he told them. "Gettin' there."

"Seams are going to be tighter than bark on a tree," one of the old-timers said. "When are ya caulkin'?" they asked.

"Hard sayin,'" Owen said.

"Ayuh," they answered back. Not once did anyone mention a

marina or selling the properties or new developments. They were all grateful for the here and now of watching them work.

One of the spectators had asked about caulking. In the past, caulkers were skilled men who arrived at shipyards with the idea they would work fast and efficiently. They were going to need to start caulking the seams of each plank below midships starting from the bottom up. As the planking was now well above midships, Susannah had seen the speed, strength, and efficiency with which the men carried the steaming planks higher and higher above ground. They had thrown together some makeshift ramps and jury-rigged platforms. Owen had seen her nearly stumble one day as a hot plank was heading for the bow area. The schooner's bow hung over the river's edge and the rocks below. He had discussed it with Kip, not her, but he did not want her planking any higher. Even though some of the men were struggling with carrying the heavy planks and keeping their balance, Susannah was quite frankly the weakest link. She was eventually coaxed to take a new job as chief caulker.

It was traditionally a coveted job, and Neville had been one of the most sought-after caulkers in St. Vincent, where caulking was one of the tasks he was first given as a teenager from his father. Neville explained that she would need to use a betel to drive wedges (irons) into the seams between each plank to open them up before caulking. He then showed her how to roll the cotton and oakum together in the palms of her hand, so it looked like a long, fibrous rope.

He then demonstrated how to stuff fibers into the seams between the planks using a handheld caulking iron. He told her to push the fibers into the seams and then take the mallet, which looked like a croquet mallet, and start the tap, tap, tap that pushed the blended fibers deep into the seams of the planks. Eventually they would remove the wedges, and the fibers in the seams would later be filled with putty, followed by layers of paint.

At first, Susannah was slow and a little demoralized. Beginning from the ground up, she spent many days on her knees near the keel. Spring thaw made it muddy, dirty, and miserable down on the ground. As she crawled along, she kept dropping the roles of oakum and cotton, and with the fibers unraveling behind her, it looked as if her intestines were spilling out in the mud. But she kept tapping at it and gathering up the "guts" again and filling the seams. Without the cotton and oakum filling the seams, Neville told her, water would seep through the planks and the boat would surely sink.

"You are doing God's work, Sue girl," he would say. "Cheese on bread! Good work!"

Neville would occasionally pick up the slack, and he worked with the speed and skill of a master. To keep her going, he told her that she was blessed with a gift and would probably always find work in St. Vincent as a caulker if she ever visited. He praised her great eye-hand coordination for the job. Soon enough, Neville left her to it and returned to planking. He simply did not need to help her as she was extremely adept, he had discovered. Eventually, Neville hung an old radio beneath some scaffolding nearby so she could listen to music while she caulked. He always had the radio tuned to a Portland reggae station, so all through the caulking she found herself catching the rhythm and soothing tones of Neville's favorite music while she worked. Somehow, her years of playing tennis meant that she could swing the caulking mallet with the precision and strength of a Wimbledon star. The men could hear but not see her working as they were always planking way above her. She was still below midships. From above, they occasionally called down to her to see how she was doing.

"Tending to the sweet lines?" someone asked one day while she was caulking and humming along to the music. She looked up thinking it was Owen, but then spotted the red stocking cap and dark brown eyes smiling down at her.

She smiled back, and he said, "Finest kind!"

She credited her caulking skills and concentration with a newfound confidence she felt in the shipyard. She stopped worrying so much about Owen and what he thought. She was good at her job, and the idea of having a set of tools and being in demand for one's skills was a wonderful feeling. There was a lot of boat to finish, and she had a knack for caulking.

CHAPTER SIXTEEN

Susannah was busy caulking when she heard a car drive up and caught a glimpse of a woman wearing a lovely woolen shawl, linen slacks, and black leather boots getting out of a black car. The woman spotted Susannah and waved hello. Today they were planning to install the ship's rudder. Susannah had blogged about this over the past week.

"Is this where Owen Dodd lives?" the woman asked as she delicately tried to avoid the deepening mud that had come with the spring thaw. "I'm Abby Tanner, from the *Boston Examiner*." The *Examiner* was a family-owned, award-winning daily newspaper read throughout New England, and she had come up from Boston looking for a good, possibly award-winning, story. She explained she had left voice messages and sent emails to Owen Dodd. Unfortunately, Owen often forgot to check messages on his land phone, and Susannah did not read Owen's emails, so she had no idea this woman was trying to reach him, had decided on coming, and was expecting to be shown the ropes after the long trip.

"Just curious, but how did you find out about Owen Dodd?" Susannah asked.

The Boston journalist had assumed Susannah was an Ossonet local and almost seemed protective of her sources. She responded in a complacent tone, "I did some extensive research on shipbuilding. Why, do you work here?"

"I do!" Susannah decided to take credit where credit was due, since the blog was being widely read and drawing more people to come and have a look. "Have you read my blog?"

It seemed the woman had not heard her and was looking over at the men.

"Your blog?" she responded, "I don't think so. I did research on the town's history." Fact was Abby had found out about *Downriver with Dodd* one evening while surfing the Internet. "Do you mind if I look around? Take a few notes?" Abby asked.

Susannah explained that it might not be a great day, as the rudder was going in, but Abby put up her hand to stop her from talking as her attention was diverted by the man walking towards them. Kip was heading toward the shipyard to begin work. He was an attractive sight coming up the road that way, but Susannah did not think it merited an open hand telling her to be silent.

Assuming it was the famous shipwright, Owen Dodd, Abby watched Kip make his usual long strides up the road. Kip walked past the two women and tipped his hat. "Morning, ladies," he said to them both in a cheerful manner.

They both watched him, and Susannah did not bother to explain to her that it was not Owen. Abby had a long-lensed camera with her and put it up to her eye and took a photo of Kip as he swung his betel off his shoulder and placed it and his tool belt on the ground near the ship. Kip then ran a gloved hand along the side of the vessel, almost patting it like a big animal. They both watched as he seemed to be having a conversation with someone on the other side of the vessel. Without asking, Abby decided to walk down and was now under the scaffolding of the vessel.

"Do you mind if I talk to you, Owen?" the reporter asked him. "I am working on a feature story."

"I'm Kip," he explained.

"Oh! He's the artist from New York, right?" she said, turning to Susannah for confirmation, while fumbling for her pen and notebook to begin an interview. She had unwittingly revealed that she read Susannah's blog. Abby didn't wait for an answer. She walked further towards the stern of the boat, looking for Owen apparently.

Susannah put her caulking material in the barn, out of the mud. She realized that this journalist was not going to listen to her or consider the part she played in this big scoop she was working on. Susannah was disappointed by her attitude but figured she better keep Abby away from the construction site for her own safety. That was always an unwritten rule in the Dodd yard—that visitors needed to stay out of harm's way, as the place was a lawsuit waiting to happen.

"Hello, who are you?" Owen asked as he nearly bumped into the reporter. He had been talking to Kip. They were waiting for a larger truck with a crane to arrive within the next half hour to help them lift the rudder and put it into place.

"I'm Abby Tanner," Abby said.

Owen didn't like landlubbers in the yard as he always worried, and he was a little annoyed when he realized that her black sedan took up valuable parking space reserved for the incoming truck. And now she was under the boat!

"Susannah, can you hold off caulking until we get the rudder in?" he called to her in the barn. Susannah nodded yes. Then, when he got closer, he whispered, "Tell her to move her goddamn car."

After moving her vehicle, Abby asked if she could talk to Owen while they waited for the truck. Susannah watched them walk together. Abby was taking notes and recording his words. Susannah admired her outfit with her linen slacks and earthy shawl that looked warm and elegant. Abby moved around the ship with an air of confidence and style. The Boston journalist was a pro and did her work while being able to negotiate the mud and still look feminine, while Susannah, by comparison, lagged behind in her mud-soaked clothes. Unfortunately, because she had to work on her knees more often as a caulker, the elbows of her coat were torn and black with dirt.

The rudder weighed about 4000 pounds, constructed by Kip and Owen on the barn floor. Rudders on a schooner were massive, moving objects that had to be big to enable a large vessel to steer. Ever since the sinking of the Titanic—where it is debated the rudder was too small—shipwrights had spent a lot of time talking about steerage and the size, shape, and weight of the rudder. In this case the rudder was massive. Installing this unwieldy yet vital piece meant they had to hire a crane operator to do it right—lift the weighty piece from its spot on the barn floor, strap it to a crane hoist, then drag it outside, where the crane would work almost like a wrecking ball hurtling towards the schooner. The trick was the men would use ropes to stop it from swinging and then lower it down into place on the stern where two heavy bronze pins were needed to fit into large bronze straps along the heel of the rudder.

Susannah had hoped to assist but was instead assigned to keep tabs on their visitor, who was pleased she had a scoop like this one for her paper and explained she would also film it on the *Examiner's* live streaming page.

"Please don't get too close." Susannah gently prevented Abby from walking ahead. "Better we stand right here." She pointed to the edge of the barn. "Do not step down and get under the ship. Don't go past the edge of the barn."

Wind gusts were coming off the river, making it hard to hear, but the gusts also turned out to be a factor in what happened next. The truck with the crane arrived, and Owen explained what he needed them to do. The crane operators were in place. The shipwrights deftly ran two huge straps around the rudder so the crane could then hoist it high above the schooner. Owen had climbed up high on the frames near the stern and was preparing to guide it into its spot. Susannah explained this to Abby in a whisper, who then repeated it on her video, giving the moment a bit more drama.

"This is going live now on all our social media outlets," Abby said. She was holding her phone and speaking into a small headset.

Once attached to the straps, the crane motor revved up, and the unwieldy rudder came swinging out of the barn, resembling a flapping ear of a giant elephant with all 4000 pounds of it gaining momentum with the swinging crane. On Owen's command, they moved it over to the stern of the schooner and high above Owen's head. The crane operator tried to swing it forward so they could steady it over the schooner and lower it while Owen was set to guide it into the pins.

"Bring it over more to the port side!" Owen shouted to the crane operator.

The shipwrights were below and had ropes to steady the movement. From their angle, they could see where it needed to be and collectively yelled "To port! To the left! Watch the wind, though! Watch out!" All their anxious shouts were heard loud and clear across the Internet as the *Examiner* reporter documented it on a live stream.

Suddenly, the crane operator shifted gears too quickly, and the momentum swung the hanging rudder quite hard, much like the seat on a Ferris wheel swings after a sudden stop. There was enough force from the wind and momentum to swing the rudder too far, too low, and too fast.

Shouts of "Rudder! Owen, rudder!" rang out. The suspended rudder and the jerky movements by the crane operator meant that the rudder was now coming full force in the direction of Owen's head.

"Duck!" Seb shouted. "Duck! Rudder!" And as the crane operator scrambled to reverse the rudder's momentum, without flinching or changing his expression, Owen expertly went into a full tuck as the rudder swung like a giant pendulum right over his head. As he crouched down, balancing on his small bit of ledge on the vessel like a downhill skier, all of those online witnessed his near miss. He was then viewed by millions as he looked up, and of course saw the rudder swinging back at him in the other direction, and without any particular care or alarm, he ducked again in a similar nimble way.

"Steady it!" he shouted to the crane operator. At the same moment ten pairs of hands shot up and grasped at the ropes to steady it, or at least slow it down. They all managed to restrain it with lines, and the rudder finally stopped moving. They then successfully lowered it and fit its pins into place with Owen guiding it from high up in the stern.

"Made! Made!" Owen shouted when it was in place. It was on a huge hinge, which he moved slightly to port and slightly to starboard with the help of a makeshift tiller, and someone shouted, "Heh, it works!"

The whole process took only about four minutes. Seb was a bit shocked by the near miss and scolded the crane driver, saying Owen's head could have "been all stove to hell" if the rudder had swiped by his skull. What most of the viewers saw was how cool and casual Owen was under pressure and Seb's accurate comment to Owen also became part of the popular viral video.

As things settled, Owen decided to do some speechifying and the viral world heard every word: "First rule of thumb in the Dodd shipyard, when you hear someone yell 'Rudder, duck,' you duck." The rudder was also the star of the show. The fine joinery and attention to details on the rudder, after closer look, resembled a beautiful piece of folk art. Owen was pleased he had Kip build most of it. "Finest kind," he said admiringly.

Abby stuck around the rest of the day, staying for lunch, talking to all the men while they in turn took a moment to rewatch the video. The views clicked upward throughout the day, and within a few days they had surpassed all expectations on social media. They had "gone viral."

It was a stunning bit of video footage followed a few days later by Abby's article, which got top billing on the front page of the Boston paper. It was a long article, and Abby borrowed rather liberally from many of the posts Susannah had written in her blog. The story went on to praise the town for all its support of shipbuilding and mentioned the wonderful meals the townspeople were bringing to support the effort. She wrote of the intriguing way they were reviving a tradition and the importance of the shipbuilding legacy to Ossonet. Abby mentioned how the culture, language, and mannerism were revived in the process. She did get the right message across but mentioned Susannah in passing, not as a caulker or worker but the person who served the men meatloaf at lunch.

CHAPTER SEVENTEEN

The *Boston Examiner* was available for sale in Clydebank, and Susannah decided to get it and show the story to her editor. He suggested he meet her near the old office. She was anxious to get there and then head back to start caulking, but she ended up getting to Clydebank at least an hour before her meeting. She was wearing her boatyard work clothes, not the best outfit to wear when meeting up with her boss, but it was too late to go back and change.

She had time to kill so after getting a stack of Boston newspapers, she decided to go to a popular coffee shop for breakfast. As she walked in, she passed a couple of the booths that were filled with teenaged girls sitting close together. She headed for the counter, wedging herself next to an older fisherman. As she sipped her coffee, waiting for the food, she noticed the girls were having a kind of powwow, whispering with their heads bent forward in a huddle. They all had mid-length straight brown and blond hair and looked like they were probably high school juniors.

As she ate, a bit of egg yolk landed on her work overalls which were already covered with linseed oil splotches, embedded wood chips, paint and dried yard mud. She was wearing her steel-toed work boots and had a bandana tied around her neck. She had forgotten about the black, torn elbows of her coat. She smiled at the thought of her transformation from a kind of cultural observer to a bona fide shipyard worker.

She was startled out of her reverie when someone sat down next to her, saying in a thick Maine accent that he was starving and wanted the breakfast special. He sat close to her at the next stool, and the movement meant that her stool creaked and toppled a bit, and she inadvertently splashed coffee on her muddy work clothes. The slight commotion caught the attention of the high school girls.

"Oops," the waitress said, and Susannah thought nothing of it. She wiped the coffee across her pant leg, where it blended in with the egg, the oil, and the dirt embedded in her clothes. She then overheard one of the teenaged girls say, "How do you know she is homeless?"

"Just look at her," the other girl said. "Her pants. Eeew."

She heard giggles, and the loud whispering grew. She realized they were laughing and pointing at her.

"She looks like a hobo," one of them said. "A fat hobo."

"Weirdo," another whispered. "She is gross."

Susannah finished her breakfast and paid quickly. She pushed open the door and left the restaurant as she heard the girls burst into laughter. As she stomped down the street toward her appointment with her boss, she felt ashamed. The girls had gotten under her skin.

In the shipyard, for centuries, women were obliged to watch men act, do, play, or build. Even now, when the reporter came to write about the shipyard, she only wanted to hear about the male shipwrights. Susannah felt whether it was at the Clydebank News or the Dodd shipyard, she might not ever be holding the cards, and like the matriarchal society she had stumbled upon in China, it was the ancient Mosu women sitting out in the square, but here she was in 21st century America still very much standing in the doorway.

Bill King was waiting on the corner to meet her, and when he saw her, he laughed.

He looked at her through his glasses and then over his bifocals for perspective. She was an enigma to him. Talented, a good writer but not committed at all to local journalism. Bill could not fully blame her for that, and she always met her deadlines, so he was loathe to scold her. "So, let's see this article."

She handed him the newspaper and mumbled, "It got about 1.5 million views on social media, too." Bill looked it over and nodded as he read it, studied the photos and captions.

He closed the newspaper and gave her a long, somewhat puzzled look. For a split second she thought she was going to be fired.

"You know, in this whole story, the only time you are mentioned is that you serve the men meatloaf." Bill looked a little puzzled. "How much longer until you think this boat is done?" he asked.

"Owen always says 'hard sayin', not knowin,'" but I am pretty sure it will be in the water by early June."

"It's already April! Wow. Okay. So, if this is such a big news story, why don't we do more videos from the boatyard and put a bit of your blog in a section of our website, with video? Can you do that for us? I can get Francis to cover a couple more municipal meetings."

She was inwardly delighted that writing about sewage pipes would no longer be her primary job.

"It's just a couple more months," Bill added, "and God knows we can use help with our circulation, too. Why should the *Examiner* get all the glory? In the meantime, I want you to also get me some more information about the town wanting to develop a marina. How is that going to impact your shipbuilder?"

She told him that she had gone to the Ossonet public library and found a bunch of bound documents that covered almost one hundred years of Ossonet Town Meetings, which was what she began to focus on—primarily the approval of any town bylaws. She had discovered something interesting about the Town Meeting of 1922. It was an article on the Town Warrant that stated "Article 29 of the Town Warrant henceforward puts in place a bylaw that the waterway in front of the Dodd shipyard and the nearby Gregory shipyard must remain clear for the purpose of shipbuilding and launching schooners for all time. The statute of limitations will last to protect the shipbuilding industry in Ossonet for future generations." The article received 650 votes in favor and 5 votes against. The only way to stop that would be to revisit the bylaw and add an article on the Town Warrant for its extension or reapproval at Town Meeting in June.

Bill said, "Sounds like you've got your story. Go for it! And Susannah"—he looked like a disappointed but amused parent—"what's with your coat? Have you been living outside?" Even Bill was teasing her.

CHAPTER EIGHTEEN

Susannah carried two tools now, a caulking mallet and a small video device. It was getting close to the end of the planking, and there was some talk that—as Owen had feared—they might run out of planks. Owen had told her he would be talking with Kip about the shortage that evening.

With the *Clydebank News's* blessing to do research, she started going to the Ossonet public library more often.

By now Susannah knew that a local bylaw could be challenged if an article was placed on a Town Meeting warrant and put up for vote. She wondered if Weasel Martin already knew about the old bylaw from 1922. It could be overturned and he was quite brazenly helping with the preliminary plan to build a marina. The only way for Owen to ensure they could NOT go through with their plans would be to add an article on the Town Warrant for the preservation of the bylaw.

She left the library anxious to tell Owen that the Dodds needed to submit such an article to the warrant for a spring Town Meeting vote. He was not home. It had been a warmer than usual night, and she thought he must have lingered longer at Kip's boat because of the spring weather. She knew they were likely deep into a conversation about wood.

She was passing through the old Gregory shipyard towards the town landing and Kip's boat to tell them. She did not really like walking alone through the Gregory yard at night, and as she passed one of the old Quonset-style buildings, she heard some movement behind one of the doors. She was startled by the red glow of a cigarette and assumed it was one of the rusticators. It seemed the cigarette moved sideways and then there was another long drag on it. The tip now really lit up someone's face. It was Mysterious Nick.

He was not alone. Nick had in fact been sharing a cigarette with one of the rusticators whom she didn't know that well. Susannah nodded at Nick and said a short "hi" to the man she did not know. It seemed a little strange to find them huddled together as if they were smoking off one cigarette, then she realized they were sharing a joint, and by the sounds of their laughter, they were a bit high. She walked past the room where he and Neville were lodging and could see a light on and figured Neville was home. She assumed while Nick was outside getting stoned, Neville was probably reading the Bible or writing a letter to his father in St. Vincent. She liked to imagine his quiet, pious life. Neville was such a steady influence on all of them. She had learned to wholly appreciate his West Indian credo to be giving and forgiving above all else. He seemed to not only keep the mood light around the shipyard, but he was so very proud of his island back home and spoke of their solid traditions. He also always encouraged her caulking skills. She was thinking she should tell him again how much she appreciated his help with caulking but was certainly not going to disturb his nightly prayers.

As she approached Kip's boat, she took a moment to look at the waxing moon with its light reflected on the water in the river basin. She was reminded that a waxing moon is meant to be a motivator to work harder, have more energy and ambition to get things done. The shipyard was full of that waxing energy as they were nearing the last plank and rounding the corner to a launch date. The signs of spring were everywhere. The marsh peepers and frogs were coming out, and she could hear their wonk, wonk, wonk sound out on the marsh.

When she got to where the boat was tied up and walked from the land across a small ramp to the deck of Kip's boat, she called to them and climbed down the cabin ladder. To her surprise she found Janet, Seb, Kip, Neville, Sherry, and Owen. They had apparently been smoking weed, as she could now smell it. It looked like spring was in the air on Kip's boat, too, in the form of a cozy pot party.

She could hear Neville talking about St. Vincent, but she was surprised that it was not in the way she imagined.

"So, there is no nude sunbathing allowed on St. Vincent, right?

But a lot of my friends, we do it anyway. One day, the local cop got tired of catching us and giving us one warning after another. They decided to make an example of me. They brought me right to the station. Naked. They brought me stark naked to the station."

They were all laughing, giggling more like it, and every one of them looked properly stoned. So much for Neville being in bed reading the Bible, Susannah thought.

She awkwardly joined them and was a little annoyed that it seemed this was a nightly thing where they gathered and smoked pot. She explained her idea about a preservation article and suggested they could submit an article to appear on the Town Warrant about protecting the waterway.

"It won't stop the town from trying to develop the area someday, but they will not get this marina anytime soon if the bylaw is held up," Susannah said.

Janet was the one who piped in here and said, "Susannah, you sound like you would make a great mayor!" She was trying to rally the rest of them.

"Selectman or selectwoman, rather," Susannah corrected her and instantly regretted sounding bitchy towards Janet. They were all trying to be less giddy and more serious. Susannah was resigned to talking to a bunch of stoners but continued. "But really, Janet, have you ever thought of running for the select board?"

Janet shook her head, no, she had not. Seb shrugged. Owen had absolutely no interest in politicians. Sherry said, "I just moved back, so no, I guess."

"You live here now so why not?" Susannah said, and could not hide a cold tone in her voice.

"Maybe I should run," Janet said. "What about you, Susannah? Aren't you a resident?"

"No," she said. None of them had realized she still had her apartment in Clydebank and was not officially living with Owen. But they all knew now, including Sherry.

It was getting late, and she was finally able to be alone with Owen, walking through the old shipyard. The moon was by now three quarters of the way across the sky. Mysterious Nick and the other man were gone, but she thought she noticed, under the metal roof of one of the sheds, the single red glow of someone taking a drag on a cigarette.

"This place seems to be full of people lurking around." She said it loudly so whoever was out there might hear her. "So, do people just come down here and hang out at night in the shipyard? I had no idea."

"I guess so." Owen shrugged.

"What about Sherry?" Susannah asked as they got closer to the house. "You never mentioned she was part of the group. When did she start coming around?"

"Just about a month ago," he noted. "She just stops by sometimes to see how the work is going on the boat. I think she might have a crush on Kip."

"Are you sure it's Kip she has a crush on?" Susannah asked, knowing she sounded petty, but she could not help herself. "Can't she just come by during the day when everyone else does?"

"Well, she has a day job. You know, like you used to have," Owen said. "Before you became a caulker." He bumped her and put his arm around her. She held his hand as they walked back but felt a little off balance.

When they got into bed that night, she reached for Owen a little too firmly, thinking he would move closer. Instead, he rolled over with his back to her. She felt very insecure in that moment, and put her hand on his shoulder and rubbed his back.

"Thanks but I am so exhausted," he tried to apologize. "I really appreciate what you found out tonight about the bylaw. That is going to buy us some time. I wonder if you would mind posting that we need more wood for the planks," and with that he started to snore and was out for the night.

Now, along with the well-meaning folks leaving a beanpot on the doorstep, people around the county started dropping off hardwoods, like oak. What they really needed were oak trees for the sawmill to make good lumber to last on the schooner for twenty-five years. They were getting lovely pieces of knotted firewood instead. They were all anxious now to finish the planking and move on to building the decks and getting her ready to go into the water. Kip had boards stored at Richardson's on Great Morse Island, which he was preserving for a planned boat of his own. Good, seasoned oak was hard to find. He somewhat reluctantly decided to offer it to Owen.

It would take two vehicles to get the planks off Great Morse Island and bring them back. Janet Gregory would drive a Chevy pickup truck and Seb had his vintage Ford truck. It was about all they needed to transport the necessary planks. Kip would go with Seb in case the truck broke down. Janet said she wouldn't mind some company for the drive. Susannah jumped at the chance to go. They would spend the night on the island and be back on the first ferry. Owen was incredibly grateful for the gesture. He told him, "I will always love you, Kip!" and Kip, feeling very conflicted by his excitement that Susannah would travel to his island and be away from Owen, could not look at him and simply mumbled back, "Ayuh."

CHAPTER NINETEEN

Susannah was glad to be on the ferry again, and although it was brisk on the water, the sun was warm and the four of them were having fun being together. It felt like a company outing.

Susannah and Janet took her truck to the inn where they were going to stay. The plan was they would meet Seb and Kip later and help load up the trucks.

The women were happy to just hang out at the inn for a while. Their room had twin beds, and Janet and Susannah each flopped down.

Janet said she hadn't been away since she had returned to Ossonet. The last time she had been in a hotel was during a romantic getaway she'd had with a Californian who took her to the wine country of Napa for the weekend. She described the way he looked, his long hair, his beard, and a flowing robe he wore like a poncho. He'd been tall and tanned and had broad shoulders.

"To be honest, Susannah, he looked a little bit like Jesus," Janet said. They got laughing at that visual.

"You spent a weekend drinking wine with Jesus?" Susannah asked, laughing.

"The worst part is, I haven't really had sex with anyone since Jesus."

"I'll pray for you, Janet."

Susannah seemed to be having the opposite problem. She was happy to have her man but struggled to put into words why being with Owen was beginning to feel like her time with the anthropologist, Eric.

"I think I've been going about this all wrong, Janet." She

complained about the reporter doing that story in the Examiner, who interviewed everyone but her, then described her as someone who "only made meatloaf."

"Yeah, I read that," Janet said. "Owen must have filled her in on all the work you were doing?"

"Not so sure about that," Susannah said. "I think whatever it was, she had a set idea about me or my role. I know in some ways what she was after. It's not easy to tell this whole story and then say, 'Oh, by the way, there is a reporter who actually lives with the shipwright documenting the whole thing.' Maybe it was better to just relegate me to the stove."

"Maybe easier but not accurate," Janet said, making a good point. Susannah then told her about her embarrassing incident at the diner in Clydebank and how the teenage girls reacted to her.

"It's like when I was a little girl, I wanted to be a cowboy," Janet said. "So, my mother got me a cowgirl outfit for my seventh birthday. I proudly wore that outfit to school, complete with my fringe skirt, my cowboy boots, my tasseled shirt, and cowgirl hat. From the moment I got on the school bus to the end of the school day, I was teased and harassed by the boys and pointed at by the girls. As soon as I got home, I put the cowgirl outfit away and never wore it again. Sometimes I wonder if it's why I ended up going out west. I still wanted to be a cowgirl."

"And you are a cowgirl in a lot of ways," Susannah said. She had her own story. "I had always wanted to be a carpenter growing up. I wasn't quite sure what that involved, but I tried to build a rabbit hutch once. My best friend and I kept nailing boards together the wrong way and could not make it into a square. Our parents gratefully accepted an offer from a local father and his sons to build us one. They literally took the hammers away from us and handed them to the boys. What is funny is that years later, a friend who did become a carpenter said he was working on a job and found my name carved into the wood of an old garage that was being torn down. It said 'Susannah Pierce, carpenter.' I was nine years old."

"We knew our calling all along!" Janet said.

"I think what I did growing up was that I gave up on things. It is so easy to quit something."

Suddenly Janet blurted out, "I want to be a selectman. I want to run for selectman in Ossonet during the June elections. That's what I want, or maybe that is what I think the town needs."

Susannah answered, "The town needs you! You have my vote; even though I am not a resident of Ossonet."

Janet asked, "Maybe you can help me with some publicity?"

"Of course," Susannah said. "Maybe from now on we just go with what feels right and act." She was feeling better.

"We better go over to Kip's as I think there will be food there," Janet added.

"Yeah, I'm starving," Susannah said. "Let's go."

Janet and Susannah were both pleased to see Seb dressed up for dinner in his clean blue jeans and a blue Oxford shirt. The shirt looked starched, new, and a little too tight, but it must have been a special occasion kind of shirt, as the women had never seen it before. He had brushed his unkempt hair back and wore a clean cap. As Seb had also been featured in the Examiner story and video, one of the guests greeted him but said at first glance he had not realized who he was. Janet and Susannah shared an amused look when Seb pointed to his clothes and straightened his cap and said, "You might not recognize me in these 'going ashore' clothes. I usually look more like the fag end of a hurricane. Don't look that way tonight, though. No, sir."

Seb had undergone an interesting change since those early days when he was scaring off volunteers with his glass eye routine. And even though they had both tried to hide it, it seemed the shipyard's revival had drawn Janet and Seb to each other and there was a fondness growing between them. There was a ten-year age difference, but Janet was a bit of a wise old soul, and they now shared a desire to preserve their town's shipbuilding history. Susannah figured if Janet were to become a selectperson, that would really keep her from heading back out West. Susannah enjoyed watching them together as they inched their way toward looking and acting more and more like an item.

Kip's parents had planned a small party that evening unbeknownst to the four travelers, so it was a nice time to talk to their neighbors and family friends who had spent summers on Great Morse Island. They spoke of Kip like Ossonet people spoke of Owen in that he was their native son, and they were proud of him. They had all read the *Boston Examiner* article and/or seen the video of the rudder he had built. They, too, were intrigued by Owen Dodd. When one of the neighbors realized Susannah lived with Owen, they asked her to tell them more about him.

So, on her one evening away from Owen in many months, Susannah spent much of the evening dutifully fielding questions about him. At one point, Susannah recognized a woman there whom she had met New Years Eve and inched towards Claire MacInnis who was interested in talking to her.

Claire told Susannah that she loved the blog and "was at first surprised you got out there planking and caulking, but I am glad you did."

Claire then said to Susannah that "Owen Dodd must be a pretty special character."

Susannah repeated the story she had been telling the other guests about how Owen had been studying all of these techniques, but until this year, no one had built anything in the Ossonet style for seventy-five years.

Claire said, "And it's too bad that there is so little demand for more of them. Most customers today want modern vessels with newer shipbuilding techniques. They want the look of tradition, but also all the bells and whistles."

Susannah joked, "Yeah, right now there is only one bell in the yard, and that is the one we ring for mug up."

"He is lucky to have you helping him; I hope he knows that!" Claire said.

"No, he doesn't really notice me!" Susannah said and realized she had blurted out something on her mind. "Sorry! I shouldn't have said that."

"What happens on Great Morse Island stays here," Claire joked.

As they were leaving the house to go back to the inn, Janet was saying good night to Seb, who was bunking with Kip at the house.

Susannah waited for Janet and stood with Kip in the dooryard. She had not realized he was listening to her conversation with Claire.

"Owen does notice," he stressed. "I think he just doesn't want to play favorites."

She shrugged. "Maybe that is why he is tough on me in the shipyard. I just don't think he feels lucky to have me. Maybe he does believe that old superstition that women are bad luck in a shipyard."

They ended up walking out the door together. Kip was more

confident being home on his island. He was on an even keel with the neighbors who were artists and academics and knew businesspeople like Claire. It seemed a more stimulating place, too, than Ossonet, perhaps in part because there was not the overhanging heaviness of one or two families—the Dodds and Gregorys—dominating the past and future culture of the town.

"There is a kind of openness here that I like," she said. "This is a very cool island."

"It is a different story than Ossonet, but this is Maine through and through. Summer people, artists, and old island homes and how that all came about. I grew up with Claire as she summered here," he said.

"She is great," Susannah said, thinking somehow that Claire and Kip were meant to be.

"Claire is kind of a legend in Maine," Kip told her. "In a different way, but we all sort of see her shipbuilding business as cutting edge."

"It's kind of hard to believe that there is a cutting edge in this business." Susannah did not know about the composite materials, lightweight metals, and advanced computer graphics that went on at MacInnis's.

He gave her a reassuring rub on her shoulder. She was wearing a heavy coat, but his hand felt very warm on her back. He then pulled her in a bit closer for a short hug good night. The hug lasted a bit longer than it should have.

"Can I ask you to come and see me tomorrow early?" Kip asked.

"Tomorrow? Before the ferry?" Susannah asked. She convinced herself Kip might have something like a spare tool for her to take to Owen. Yet, she instinctively knew it was a riskier kind of invitation.

The following morning, Susannah got up very early and packed, leaving a note for Janet to head down to Richardson's before they went to the ferry.

She felt fresh from sleep and a night away from home. She walked to the shop and entered through a big wooden door. Kip had been looking around for a tool, so she greeted him by handing him a coffee. His face was clean shaven, and there was a scent of shaving cream mixed with the linseed oil and fresh wood and the salty smell of an onshore breeze.

"Is there anyone else here?" Susannah asked.

"No," Kip said. "I wanted you to come by as I was going to show you a painting I am working on if you want to go down below." Kip pointed towards the boat in a matter-of-fact way. Without a word, she climbed up the ladder of the boat, and then went to the cabin. She was excited by being there alone and waiting for him. He went to the barn door and latched it and then climbed on board. They were alone in the cabin and with limited time before Janet or Seb came by to get them to the ferry. They leaned against the navigational station which was like a small desk. He put down his coffee and while remaining dressed they rapidly explored, touched one another. She felt electrified when he reached down into her underpants and penetrated her with his fingers with one hand and stroked her breast with his other. She lifted her arm and stroked his hair which was thick as a rope. Her extended arm allowed her to arch herself so he could stroke her body while pulling, almost tugging her pants down and returning his hand to her clitoris. She let go of his hair and began unbuckling his belt. She moved her hand so that she felt his penis, and that contact prompted them to both move farther back into the cabin towards a bunk.

As they moved, he pulled her shirt and bra off and her large breasts brushed his neck and face as they lay down. He said, "Oh my God, they are beautiful." She ran her hands down his backside while he ran his hands down the front of her and then put his warm hands on her ass as it was a bit cold on the bunk. He dropped his jeans and pulled off his shirt as she kicked off her panties. Breathing hard, he lay on top of her. She was lost in the heat of his male physique, the one she had been rubbing up against while planking all winter and sitting close to while having lunches each day and feeling, responding to his nearness all along. She had been watching him and learning about him and admiring him for months. It felt almost natural that he was about to be inside her as he had been by her side all along it seemed. She wanted this moment so badly that she did not listen to her conscience and could only hear him speaking in a beautiful language she could not understand.

As he made love to her, it felt as if the boat were sailing and all she could hear was a soft wind and the sounds of their pleasure. As he coaxed her to climax, she felt she was rolling downwind— a graceful state of sail that feels like surfing a wave. While she was usually self-conscious about calling out and making noise when reaching orgasm, this time she heard her own voice reach beyond recognition, which was a sensation she had never, ever experienced before. She had no idea if he had already come inside her because moments after she came, she felt she was sailing again, reaching orgasm a second time as he pressed himself deeper inside her. He said with urgency "*Atteindre le point culminant.*" She had no idea why he was speaking French but it made it easier to forget everything else as they climaxed together. For a few precious moments afterwards, she imagined they were heading southeast on a sail towards Guadeloupe with no time constraints, and no one to answer to.

Kip did, however, look at his watch and it was almost time to get to the ferry, yet they could not stop kissing, touching and finally laughing and trying to get up. As they scrambled down out of the boat, they both knew they were going to hell but what a liberating ride it was getting there!

She could hear the vehicles of Janet and Seb pulling up. They were talking outside and heading for the door. Kip, now dressed and putting on his hat, walked to the barn and flung open the door to greet them with a smile. As the sun poured into the barn, it turned out he had startled a barn owl who had been nesting in the rafters. With the door now open, the owl took flight and Kip ducked as it nearly dive bombed him before soaring out over the water.

CHAPTER TWENTY

Throughout maritime history, it is believed to be good luck for strong drink to be poured over the last plank as it marks the completion of the hull. The final plank—or whiskey plank—is marked by a whiskey plank party, a true occasion that must be noted with strong whiskey and speechifying, according to Owen. They had now used up all the planks from Great Morse Island and had one plank to go. Owen was ready. "Plank coming out!" Owen shouted, and then added for good measure, "Plank coming out! Last one!"

Kip and Neville, wearing their oven mitt gloves, were asked to pull the last plank out of the box. Seb, Quinn, Mysterious Nick, and Susannah each took a corner and carried it toward the schooner.

They scrambled with it up the scaffolding toward the bow as fast as they could. Susannah was amazed at how high up they were, on the precarious outer edge of the vessel. As the wood cooled, Owen clamped it down easily, Kip drilled holes, and then the two of them held their mallets high, pounding the trunnels into the side of the beautiful whiskey plank. Owen then used the power drill to ram the bronze screws in so that the vessel would remain, for at least a decade or two, as tight as a drum.

Owen wiped the sawdust and bits of dirt off the whiskey plank with his hand. Running his hands over the final plank, he turned toward the small crowd and shouted, "The whiskey plank is made! It's done!"

Owen poured the whiskey over the plank and then took a swig from the bottle.

"Huzzah!" He coughed a bit, took one more swig and handed

the bottle to Seb. One by one, each shipwright took a swig, poured some onto the plank, and passed it on. Susannah had her turn as well. They polished off that bottle and cracked open another. It was a single malt bottle of the famous Glenlivet Scotch.

"Wow!" Kip said. "A single malt? That is classy!" He took a sip and passed it to Susannah, who had also been documenting the whole thing with a small video camera. Since the plan was the final plank would go in on a Saturday, they had asked thirty or so people to come for a private celebration.

Looking around at the people below watching the whiskey plank go on, she heard someone mumble.

"That's it?" the person asked.

Susannah looked at Owen and said, "Is that it? Any speeches?"

This was a little different from the keel-laying and tree lighting in that she was engrossed in the boat and had not really been thinking about having an audience. But there they all were.

"No more speeches until we putty, paint, and launch her!" Owen said. "Let's get her done."

Some local shell fishermen had donated a few bushels of clams, and one of his Clydebank friends traded him fifteen lobsters for a promised sail. Owen had been thinking of how to pay back the shipwrights and wanted a good clambake, even if it was a bit early in the season for that.

But it looked like Kip and Seb were leaving.

"Just goin' down the road a piece," Seb explained to Owen.

They returned soon after with Seb driving his pickup and Kip beeping the horn.

They pulled the truck right up to the firepit. Kip and Seb unloaded a large, flat piece of a cast iron grill. They put it down over a portion of the fire and Kip held up a huge side of beef.

"Papa Jawsus!" said Neville. "Break my heart, Kip!"

Kip had been thinking about this surprise for months, especially for Neville, as he knew that no one liked a barbecue as much as Neville. Ever since they had known each other, Neville always reminded Kip that the word barbecue originally came from the Caribbean. Neville used to explain that a now vanished tribe called the Taino used the word barbacoa to describe grilling on a raised wooden grate. He was delighted that Kip had thought of bringing the grill and the meat.

They laid the large rib on the grill. The rusticators had been working on building a perfect fire, and they had brought out a few big pots for boiling the lobsters and steamers.

"I've been saving these cedar wood chips for an occasion such as this," Kip said, and proceeded to sprinkle the scented chips over the fire.

"Don't feed those chips to my lobsters," Owen warned.

By mixing his cedar chips with the hard wood already burning, the fat dripping on the wood gave off a sweet, mouth-watering charcoal smell. "And keep those bugs away from my cow," Kip answered back. As they stood together, Susannah took a photograph of Owen and his lobsters and Kip beside his beef. She'd managed to capture them in the same frame and later reposted the photo, adding a little side story about combining the flavors of land and sea on one plate, commonly called "surf and turf."

The meat was so tender, Kip said they could cut it with a spoon. He doled pieces out to shipwrights. It was all so good that the fat got all over everyone's mouths and hands, and the lobster juice dripped down their chins. They were too busy eating to wipe it away.

After a while, Neville, surely no longer the quiet man Susannah thought him to be, stood up to sing his calypso. This West Indian tradition was a bit of a story set to a tune and was likely a version of a sea shanty. Neville could carry a tune, but the tin-like ripple of the steel drum was missing.

"'Frame by frame, the sea will hold her, plank by plank, the sea won't fold her; she will be in St. Vincent town with me aboard her... She and I will never argue, she and I will never cry," Neville sang. "She and I will never die."

"Nice song, Nev!" Owen said. "You are all welcome to sing as much as you want. I just make one request. Please, no accordions."

They all laughed, knowing Owen had a strong aversion to the sound of a squeeze box. For him, it was like howling cats.

"You need to come to the Caribbean, mon," Neville told Owen. "We have the soft sounds of calypso, steel drums, rum. You gotta sail there!"

"I want to see 100,000 islands," Owen nodded. "Flung like jewels upon the sea."

"Heh, that is good," Neville said.

"Yeah, not mine." They both knew it as a classic sailing song.

Sitting on a log for an extended period got uncomfortable for some, and whoever had a better seat lost it if they got up and ended up having to sit on a log next to someone else. As there was plenty of food and drink to finish, they were tripping over each other, laughing, and playing a kind of musical chairs until there was no place to sit. Eventually, out of the corner of her eye, Susannah spotted Sherry who had momentarily landed on Owen's lap and was still there.

Janet was now talking with Seb, and one of the rusticators had gotten up to sit next to Mysterious Nick. She wondered if it was Nick's smoking buddy. Susannah's mobile phone was ringing and she was able to adeptly remove Sherry from Owen's lap by telling Owen that Abby, the reporter from the Boston Examiner, was on the phone. Abby had wanted to keep tabs on the boat, so Susannah had let her know when the whiskey plank celebration would be taking place. Owen walked away from the fire so he could talk to her on the phone. They could hear Owen speaking about how he was tearing up the steam box tomorrow. "Going into the charter trade this summer," he told Abby. "Sure, we can head to Boston easily by boat."

Susannah didn't know until that moment Owen was going to go into the charter business. She looked around to see if anyone else had heard it. Kip was looking into the fire and smoking a hand-rolled cigarette. He was not listening to Owen's call. She thought Kip was staring into the flames, because she could not see his eyes clearly through his burning cigarette and the smoke of the outdoor fire. They had been avoiding each other since returning from Great Morse Island and were very much acting as if nothing happened between them. But as he took a drag on his hand-rolled cigarette, she could see more clearly where he was looking. Kip was gazing intently at her and when a flicker of light from the fire highlighted his face, the look he had made her feel like he was pulling her arm over arm over the fire to be closer to him. She stared at his smoldering eyes. He took another drag on his cigarette and rubbed his face with his free hand. It was warm by the fire, and he took off his red stocking cap. She loved to watch how all that thick hair tumbled out of it. With his face somewhat hidden by his hair, he continued to watch Susannah watching him. A lump was rising in her throat. She wanted to be sitting near him. The interview between Owen and Abby meandered, and finally Owen hung up and bounded back to the fire. He started in on a sea shanty.

"Well, it's all for me grog, me jolly, jolly grog. It's all for me beer and tobacco! For I spent all me tin on the lassies drinking gin, far across the western ocean I must wander."

After many stanzas Owen got to the last line— "Where is me bed, me noggin noggin bed? All gone for beer and tobacco!"—and bumped into Susannah, who stumbled a little as she edged toward the open seat next to Kip. Owen then asked "Kip! What are the words?"

She caught Kip's eye again, and they both smiled and shook their heads as if to say, "Owen is too much tonight!" Kip stood up and shouted along to the tune, "And me ass is looking out for better weather!"

Over on the other side of the fire, Owen still spinning and singing again, "Where is me bed. Me noggin, noggin bed . . ."

Bed was the best place for him, so when Owen headed inside 'just for a minute,' and they all could hear a crashing sound, they knew he was done for the night. Seb went in. He called out a window, "He's okay!" He then slammed down the window, and they could still hear the muffled sounds of Owen's singing until he finally fell asleep. The party started to disperse, but Sherry hung on quite late.

Finally, Seb got up and said he was going to head to the shanty. Kip called out to Seb, "I'll be right over, Seb. I'm just wanting to make sure this fire burns down first." Kip walked over to the fire and assessed it. After that, he went to find his gear, and Susannah noticed that Sherry followed him into the barn. She would not interfere with anything Sherry was up to. How could she?

Susannah felt quite alone as she watched the two of them disappear into the barn. Yet why shouldn't a single man be in the barn at midnight with Sherry when they were both likely a bit drunk, a bit lonely?

Susannah went inside to check on a sleeping, snoring Owen. She covered him with a blanket, and from inside she watched the campfire outside burn down. She noticed that the barn remained pitch dark. She imagined it were her in that barn. She could imagine Kip walking up behind her, and he would caress her as they leaned into a beam in the barn. They would move into the far end of the loft and embrace against the big window frame. She imagined their view—the river and the schooner silhouetted by the large spring moon. She could feel him pulling her down to the loft bench and they would then begin to make love.

Suddenly, a car pulled up and she could see the little Uber sign. Sherry must have called for a ride. The Uber tooted a few times, and no one came out of the barn. Susannah decided she better let Sherry know, so she hustled over to the barn and called up to the big open loft on the second floor.

"Kip? Kip, there's a ride here for Sherry."

Nothing.

Susannah decided she'd better go check on them. She climbed up the barn steps, lit only by slivers of the full moon. "Kip? Sherry?" As she approached them, it occurred to her that Kip was alone, sound asleep on the wooden bench. They had all been very close to the wood smoke and greasy food all evening, so he must have taken off his work shirt. A shaft of moonlight cut across his torso.

Susannah smiled at his sleeping self. She decided to lean in closely just to make sure he was breathing. She kissed him on the face. When she did, he woke up.

She pulled back, saying, "I am sorry. You were asleep."

Kip smiled up at her, "No, I was awake." He sat up.

She could hear a little toot of the car. "I thought Sherry was in here!" Confused and a bit offended, Kip asked, "Sherry?!"

She went back down and told the driver to try the other yard. She also gave him $30 and a paper plate of food for his trouble. She did a quick check on Owen, who was out cold. Instead of going to bed, she returned to the barn. She ran up the loft stairs and whispered to him that she just wanted to say good night.

"*Kesaluloq*," Kip said. "*O' mu weleyim.*" He was speaking in Micmac and was nearly asleep. He was not quite ready to speak to her in English about how he was feeling.

"Goodnight, Kip" she said not understanding a word but afraid if she came any closer she would not be able to leave.

"*Atie' wit, Ku'ku'kwes,*" he said, hearing her steps leaving the barn. "Goodnight, Owl."

CHAPTER TWENTY-ONE

Two days after the whiskey plank party, just when the late spring weather really set in as a preview to summer, Owen announced it was time to dismantle the steam box. The steam box had really become, for all of them, a cherished symbol of shipyard life; now it was headed for a scrap pile behind the barn. In a silent procession, like pallbearers, all the shipwrights helped carry it to its final resting place. The men stood looking down at the steam box like a group of mourners. The grieving did not last long as the deadline to launch the boat was approaching. Kip grabbed a little time to set up his easel and paint the scene as time allowed. His oils and watercolors featured them gathered around the steam box or lifting a frame all together or driving trunnels into the planks. He put this life they were all leading, centered around the ship, onto the canvas.

By now, Susannah had not only lost her fear of the band saw but was growing comfortable with an array of power tools, so she was asked to help "square the mast." To square the mast they had layered planks of lumber together using a strong glue and tight clamps. Once the planks were firmly stuck together, the edges needed to be squared off. She and Quinn sanded and polished off the squares until the pile of rectangular planks was turned into a smooth, round mast. Simultaneously, Neville was making the sails in the loft. Not only was he a skilled carpenter, but back in St. Vincent, he and his brothers had also been expert sailmakers.

Laying the deck was proving more complicated, as they were still using fine oak planks. Kip had to make another trip to Great Morse

Island to donate more wood while Owen was busy at the sawmill cutting a recently acquired giant timber for the deck. As they lay them down on deck, it was like the schooner had a new floor. Everyone was taking the time to walk around on the unfinished deck. At first, there was very little deck to stroll across, but eventually they got it so they could strut back and forth like Jack Sparrow on the *Black Pearl*. For days, Susannah watched Kip, Owen, and the men walk the deck, high up on the schooner, as if they were already at sea.

With so much to do, they needed a small army of volunteers to fill the seams that had been caulked. Each seam needed putty which would seal the hull from leaks. This would be the last step before the final sanding and smoothing, then finally painting the hull could begin. Puttying was a simple job that could be done quickly. It was not a job that shipwrights did per se, so historically they often just bribed locals to come and be putty brigades, the way the Amish people might come and finish a barn, with the whole community raising it together.

How to find a small army of people willing to putty? That question was soon answered when a band of young women, whom Owen eventually called the Swiss Misses, came to the rescue. It happened to be morning mug up, and the crew was taking a quick break, when a sudden splashing and screaming startled them all into walking over to the water's edge to see what was going on. To their surprise, there must have been twenty women—some wearing shorts and skimpy bathing suit tops, and a few were even topless—splashing around in the cold water on the little town beach by the landing. One of the young women waved from where she was swimming in the water and shouted, "*Bonjour*! Hallo!"

Another shouted, "*C'est* mug up?" Another pointed at Owen and called out, "*Vous êtes* Owen Dodd?" And they all started whooping and giggling.

Clearly, these young women, whoever they were, knew all about the Dodd shipyard and had come by to check things out. Meanwhile, their shrieks revealed they knew very little about Maine's notoriously cold water, as very few people swim in early summer. And at no time in recorded history did anyone ever swim topless off Ossonet's town landing. It would be talked about for years to come.

Several of the girls began swimming over to the shipyard using the breaststroke, the coldness of the water making them swim faster, their teeth chattering as they called out *"C'est* mugs up" between breaths. They were strong, athletic swimmers.

"Hallo!" they said as they completed the fifty-yard swim. The shipwrights rushed over to help them ashore. They came out of the water and reached out to shake Owen's hand, not knowing at first who was who. Quinn looked gob smacked, as he had no idea how to react to seeing so many uncovered female bodies at once.

Susannah went inside and grabbed a pile of towels for them. As they dried off and covered up a bit, they explained in their best English that they had all met at a youth hostel in Portland, Maine. They had been reading the blog! A mix of European nationalities—French, Italian, Spanish, Swiss, with French being the default lingua franca for most—many of the young women were on a break from university so were only nineteen or twenty years old. The Swiss girl spoke the best English, but Kip also tried to help with his coastal-accented French. As soon as the girls knew Kip spoke French, he became the focus of their attention as they asked rapid-fire questions about the town and the yard. For several minutes, he acted as interpreter as the two groups got to know each other.

It turned out one of them, a sailor back in northern France, had shared her enthusiasm for reading about the men of the Dodd shipyard, and all the daily tales had intrigued her fellow travelers. She'd convinced the whole group to travel north from Portland, and they were camping behind the town hall near the baseball field. They all wanted to meet the men of *Downriver with Dodd* in person and to see a real ancient schooner being built from scratch, all by hand. They had found it to be a lot warmer than they thought and had longed for a chance to cool off.

As they shivered a bit now, even after drying off, they mentioned they would like to get a close look at the schooner before leaving.

"I can do better than just show you around the yard," Owen said, grinning, as he swept his arms wide to direct their view to the beautiful schooner in front of them. "You could help us! Does anyone know how to putty?"

Owen tried to show them what he needed them to do by using his fingers. "Putty?" he said, pushing imaginary clay into the crack between the planks.

Their leader, the Swiss girl, interpreted what she thought he'd said into French for a girl standing next to her. Owen made it worse by now using his fingers to illustrate pushing something deep into a crack. One of the girls gasped and shook her head vigorously, as if to say you will not catch me dead doing that!

"No, no, no," Owen insisted. "The boat, the boat. Can you press soft clay into the seams of a schooner? Work with us? Can you girls help us today?"

The Swiss woman then conferred with the others, and Kip hovered around them to help answer any confusing questions. They understood finally and turned back to Owen. The Swiss girl said, "Ya. Ya. We putty. We help? Ya. Ya, okay?"

The girls then jumped back in the water and swam across to the town beach to get changed and store their gear in their parked vans.

Because the first person they had met was Swiss, Owen immediately dubbed them the Swiss Misses. The name stuck. And so, the Swiss Misses joined the growing chaos in the yard as they pressed on to get the boat ready to launch. The Swiss Misses proved to be hard workers and stayed long enough, over the course of two weeks, and were instrumental in completing much of the puttying of the seams of the hull. They did the work in a cheerful, straightforward way, speaking at least four different languages amongst them.

The shipwrights and rusticators also tried their best to remain nonplussed by the women's sleeveless tops and short shorts, and being older, also tried as best they could to ignore their youthful beauty and grace. They reserved their comments for the workmanship only. But they were in an old-school shipyard where women are still a novelty.

"They are very nimble with the puttying knife, and it is good to use their upper body strength to press the putty into the seams," observed Neville.

And to sound almost chaste, Owen added, "They are so careful. And meticulous. Leaning into the hull with their arms and chests each time is an important skill."

The men would all agree that they showed innovation and almost Yankee-like ingenuity. "Having one Swiss Miss hold a huge putty plate in her lap before beginning work is very smart," Seb would say. "Wicked smaht of them to lean over from where they are sitting and dip a hand into her lap for more putty. Ayuh."

"They use their legs very effectively," Owen would say at lunch, especially if Susannah was not within earshot. "Lunging across the deck and reaching over the side to apply the putty has been so helpful in finishing the upper part of the hull."

What they would not say, perhaps even to themselves is, "I need to get to Europe someday! They are stunningly beautiful. Are they all virgins?"

The Swiss Misses had politely asked Susannah if they could use the indoor toilet and often begged her at the end of the day to have a shower. The men tried not to get carried away by their thoughts that as the Swiss Misses streamed in and out of the main house, they were not somehow in there showering all together. The men were just as hot and sweaty as everyone else, but it was Quinn who was the only male in the shipyard still in his late teens. He said, "It's good they are saving water by showering together," but he was quickly growled at by his elder, male alpha dogs to zip it.

Meanwhile, while most of the shipwrights focused on finishing the deck planking, Kip and Owen had started walking around the boat a lot, assessing the shape of the hull. Like sculptors, they would then chip small chunks away with a drubbing axe and then sand and smooth out the hull.

They stood together looking at it.

"*Quelle beauté,*" Kip said as he had been speaking French more to everyone around the shipyard, which soothed his own melancholic thoughts. "Vous avez un très beau bateau." Of course, Owen only understood a few words of French, but he knew the boat looked good. Because many of the Swiss Misses spoke French, they overheard Kip and piped in. "*Très beau bateau!*"

One day when Owen and Kip were together at the far end of the boat and the girls were smiling and laughing as they worked, Owen nudged Kip and said, "You should take one of the Swiss Misses out for a boat ride. Or maybe take all of them. You and your French—you'll get a harem following you around the yard."

Kip shrugged with only vague interest.

"All so lovely with that come hither look," Owen said.

"Keep dreaming, old man," Kip said. "Besides, you have to focus on naming it."

"Who? What?" Owen was distracted.

"You have to come up with a name for your schooner if you

want me to carve it."

It was tradition for ships and large vessels to be named after a woman, and most boats to this day are referred to as she and her. In the olden times, they had a female figurehead, and that evolved into an ornate board where the name appeared on each side of the bow. Kip was the best carver and had offered way back to do it, but it was a precarious spot hanging over the bow in a bosun chair. He was anxious to get the job done.

Everyone had assumed Owen would name her Susannah. Since Owen was now the builder, owner, and its future captain, it seemed right to them that Susannah would receive the honor. Yet Owen kept delaying giving her a name, which added to Kip's growing frustration as he grappled with his feelings both for Susannah and his friendship with Owen. He did not think he could or should stay on in Ossonet much longer.

"Look, Owen, you got to get me a name so I can start working on carving it."

Days went by as they got closer to finishing the hull, and Kip knew could not leave this task much longer. Finally, hot, sweaty, irritated, and a little lovelorn, Kip pleaded with Owen when no one else was around. "Come on, Owen, when are you going to name your goddamn boat? We don't have much time, and you are going to have to find someone else if you don't make up your mind!"

An equally hot, tired, and irritated Owen snapped back, "Kip, when are you going to get off my goddamn back? Why don't you take one of those Swiss Misses out on your boat and get it on? They all adore you." Kip did not like what Owen was implying but he could not blame Owen for believing that was what they all needed or wanted.

"*Qu'on me route la pain*, Owen," said Kip, growing angry and frustrated perhaps more than he should have. "I need a break," he said, and flicked his hammer up high and instead of catching it, he let it hit the ground, like a microphone drop, and walked away.

"Wait a minute. No breaks here," Owen said. "You are on the clock."

Kip pivoted and began walking toward Owen. Owen knew that Kip had the bulk, build, and muscle to clobber him. And he knew the thought of doing so was tempting Kip right now.

"What do you want from me?" Kip blurted out. "You tell me and we'll both know."

Kip and Owen circled around each other, both startled by how angry they were and so ready to go at it.

Seb had been watching. They looked to Seb like two bulls pawing the earth and snorting at each other. He was not entirely in the dark about Kip's feelings for Susannah. Now it looked like they were about to face off in a duel with an adze and a sledgehammer. He knew shipyard brawls could happen quickly and turn ugly, and this one looked heated. He rushed over and stood between them both.

"What's all this ruction?" which was an old Maine expression. "Going at each other hammer and tongs."

Kip headed to the barn and said, "Just stop dillydallying and name the goddamn boat."

"Oh, yeah, yeah. Of course," Owen said, looking over at the curvy Swiss Misses as they leaned against the hull of his ship, using their fingers to squeeze the putty between the seams.

"I haven't figured out a name yet," he finally admitted to Seb.

"Getting goddamn hot and everything is drier than a burnt boot," Seb offered. "Got to launch soon, so name it."

CHAPTER TWENTY-TWO

Owen was in the barn loft at a drafting table taking a moment to reread his tide charts. He was looking for the exact time in June when the tide would be at its highest. To his relief, there was an astronomical high tide that fell on the afternoon of June twenty-first. That was ten days away. He rubbed his eyes and looked at it once again.

Owen had been given the estimated cost of using a mobile marine lift for a forty-ton vessel. It would cost nearly $10,000 to get it there, where it would then have to move over the lumpy shipyard down to the water's edge. The lift would have to transport the schooner back to a shipyard in Clydebank to lower the ship into the water. It would have been simpler, but using advanced, expensive machinery to transport and launch a schooner was wildly beyond their budget. They would have to launch her the old way during peak of high tide using a very risky technique called the Ossonet side launch.

"Come hell or high water," he whispered. He felt a strange twist in his gut. He knew it to be fear. Ossonet side launches were dangerous and had not been attempted since the 1940s. "This is going to be hell." But if they waited through summer for another astronomical high tide, the vessel would get increasingly dry and cracked. It needed salt water to preserve its wood.

Owen had been hard pressed to set a date for the launch as there was so much more to do. The "sides" of the vessel needed to be finished. The sides not only kept sailors safe from the sea, but they gave the schooner its lines and beauty. There were several wooden parts that were now being crafted that would add ornate beauty to the ship. There was the sternpost and curved railings that were being laid down up until the final hour. The spar was now rounded and sanded and nearly ready to become the bowsprit where it would be attached to the stemhead with a gammon iron. To add to the long list, they needed to paint her. And traditionally, most shipwrights used an enormous amount of paint on a wooden hull to seal her up tight. Owen chose to mix paint in the Ossonet way so pink paint would be the first coat. The base coats were never going to be the final color, and bubblegum pink made sense to him. The color became an endless source of curiosity. The people at the viewing platform and milling around the yard were puzzled and almost offended by the color. All Owen would say was, "Ayuh. Finest kind of schooner is a pink one." The shipwrights went along with it, and whenever they heard comments like "What're they thinking?" or "What a shame," the shipwrights would say "Happier than a clam at high tide! Nothing like a pink boat, yes sir!"

But as the pink layers dried, the next layers were far more textured. There was the beautiful Oyster White color painted up to its waterline and covering the pink. They then layered on deeper hues, leaving the hull below the waterline a nautical tone called Marblehead Green. But above the waterline, at the sheer line, they left a stripe of the Oyster White. They then did something unusual, foregoing the traditional blacks and giving it a red hue. It was called Corsica Red, and the ripples of water and sunlight were sure to sparkle against its dazzling deep cherry color. They chose Oyster White again and a stripe of blue for the trim along the line beneath the deck railings and bowsprit. The deck, the interior rails, and the cabin tops would be Oyster White too. The pink ship was now richly textured, striking against the green marsh, and ready for her life at sea. Now and then even the shipwrights would stop and stare up at her, pausing from their finishing tasks to admire her strength and beauty. As the final coats were drying, Kip got out his sketchbook. Once the boat was in the water, the masts would be put in place—or "stepped," in shipbuilding terms—after which the sails would be "bent on." Once those sails were hoisted, she would be ready to sail.

But they still had to get the ship from land to sea without any real machines to help them, just the tide, gravity, grease, and momentum.

Susannah was on the porch while Owen was pacing around upstairs. She was surprised when he joined her for a mug and sat down as he seemed to almost need her, which was an increasingly rare feeling. It was touching to her as it felt like earlier times, sitting close together. Now they were looking out at the water where a nearly finished schooner was getting ready to leave.

His hair was uncombed and sticking straight up, filled with sawdust. His glasses were smudged and cracked; he had dark circles under his eyes. He was suntanned and but now looked pale, and his lips had gone from red to a tight white color. He looked gaunt and exhausted while also trying to cope with being in the middle of a panic attack.

"High tide is Saturday at 3 p.m., June twenty-first," he said quietly, looking down. "We're going to have to launch her when the tide is at its highest. We need a huge jack to prop her up and lots of wood blocks. I must tell the guys to start gathering blocks. We then need lots of wedges."

"We drive in the wedges while at the same time"—he was gesturing with both hands and leaning to one side— "the wedges will make her tip, and she will be on the edge of the keel, like an ice skater on the edge of a blade, see?" He was trying to show her. She did not quite see it.

"She will be on this ice edge as we slowly add height to the stern. We grease the ways all around her, and God willing, she will go careening into the water on her own momentum. However, with a side launch, if she topples over to one side, I will be crushed. We also won't be able to move her, so I will be sort of buried alive."

Susannah now understood why Owen was pale. He finished his coffee and went outside to talk to the men. He was explaining the same thing to them.

"You are going to have to give her height and lots of grease to get her to budge," Kip noted. "We don't want her careening away and smashing up against the town dock and the harbormaster's boat on the other side, so I have some heavy chain and anchor to act like a brake. When she starts her ride, the chains will help steady her once she reaches the water."

"Okay, I like that," Owen said. He was an absolute jangle of nerves—clammy, edgy, cramped up, and just wanting to get away from the fear he felt. He was worried someone would get crushed by the schooner. Or the schooner would crush him. He left the group for a moment to head for the shade and coolness of the barn.

"Anyone willing to go under her and lower the jack needs to have their head examined," Mysterious Nick observed, and they all instinctively knew that none of them had any interest in volunteering to get under it.

"You know who's going to go under the hull?" Seb asked, knowing it was Owen. "It is going to take balls of steel."

Just then, Quinn arrived for work.

They all looked over at Quinn. He seemed to have grown three inches taller since the keel-laying ceremony, and his shoulders had broadened with his height. He had physically gotten stronger over the year working on the schooner and now at eighteen, he had matured and was quite a handsome young man. Nick said, "Maybe Quinn will do it, instead." After they explained the technique to Quinn, he knew how to respond. "My balls are still pretty much unbreakable. I should do it."

"You might want to think carefully about that, Quinn," Seb warned. "We are depending on you to keep your balls intact if we ever get to build another schooner. You and your balls got to keep it all going when we are gone."

"Got to start carving a name in soon. No matter what," Kip said, again sounding a little hot under the collar.

Just then, the house phone started to ring, and Owen heard in from the barn. He rushed towards the house to answer it. It was Claire MacInnis calling for Susannah. Owen shrugged and handed the phone to Susannah. Owen thought it might be about him, so he hung back and listened in.

"You are not going to believe this," Susannah said as she walked up to him, smiling.

"What?" he was a little impatient to get going now. "I am out straight today."

"That call was for me!" Susannah said, still somewhat startled by what had just happened.

"What did she want?" Owen said. "To come to the launch?"

"She wanted me to consider a freelance job. She asked if I might help create a blog for her shipyard. She had an idea I might be able to work it into a position as director of new business and marketing if I was game."

"Where?" he asked. "What?"

"It is at the Leighton-MacInnis Shipyard," she said, knowing it was about an hour away from Ossonet. "She wanted me to consider doing some work for them. Nothing definite, yet. She was just putting it out there."

"You already have a job," Owen said. He was nervous, preoccupied, and in a hurry.

"Yeah, but . . ." Susannah hesitated.

"I had no idea you were looking to work for my competition," he said to her briskly. He took it as her being disloyal.

As he left the room, she sputtered and said, "I was never looking for a job with MacInnis!" She grabbed his arm to stop him from racing away.

He shook her hand off his arm.

"I met Claire again when I was at the island getting more wood. She was so admiring of you. She wondered if I could 'build a brand' for her company as I did for you," Susannah explained as she followed him around the house from room to room as he was trying to make his escape.

"Build a brand?" He was confused. "We are building a boat, not a brand."

"Why not a brand?" she asked. "You have all the ability and skills you need to build up this business."

He seemed disgusted by the idea that he was a brand. She probably should have said a unique, authentic, and one-of-a-kind brand.

"They're in the running for jobs with clients all over the world," Susannah pointed out to him. "They have an order to build a 165-foot wooden style yacht, and she asked me to consider documenting it and creating a blog for them. She thinks it will help them get more orders. But they do not compete with what you might do next!"

"It is called cold-molded wood. They just glue laminated wood together and call it a wooden boat! You would be a total sellout!" Owen said, turning back angrily. He was now in the dooryard about to go out the front door. "What about the charter business?"

"You could grow this business—and build more yachts?" She had mistakenly said the word 'yacht' and set off a strong reaction.

He spat out at her, "I don't want to build toys for the wealthy out of fake wood. MacInnis builds shit boats, and they do shit work. Going to work for them would be a huge mistake."

His strong opinion about MacInnis hit her hard. She knew despite her attempts at anthropology and journalism and shipbuilding, this was a moment where she might just be the right person for the job.

"If you need money, I've got plans for us to make money once the boat is launched. I am going to offer charter sails this summer out of Clydebank."

"Clydebank?" she asked. She had long ago decided she didn't really like the city. It was dull and dreary.

Finally, after wanting to say it for a long time, she blurted, "I think you should try and build up your boat business first. You haven't even tried!"

"There is no goddamn future in the boatbuilding business!" And with that he was nearly out the door, seemingly for good, by the way he was talking to her.

"Look, I am just not going to work for anyone else. Not after all this work," he said. "Chartering is a business, Susannah," Owen said firmly. He was astute enough to know that he was being unfair to her, but he was too proud and too preoccupied to say it.

"So, I have no choice but to go into the charter business?" she asked.

"What if I said yes, it would help if you worked on it with me?" he asked.

"It would help you, or us?" she asked. She realized she knew the answer before asking.

Owen was outside now and looked over at the men. They all overheard her last few words, and he shrugged as if they would agree with him and said, "Geez, women!" but they did not look at him. "I need gas," he said, and they still did not look up. He sheepishly got in his car, saying nothing. He accelerated so fast up the hill that he had to slam on the brakes at the top of the road. They could all hear the car accelerate onto the main road out of town. They heard the loud horn of a passing truck as if Owen had nearly caused an accident.

"What just happened?" Susannah asked herself, feeling tempted to pack up and drive away herself.

She turned away from the porch window, aware that all the shipwrights were within earshot. She did not want to face them and gently shut the front door.

As she looked around her, she spotted, in the corner of the

room, an old navigational chart on the floor. Owen must have been plotting a course for the schooner, but on the paper chart it appeared there was a narrow sea route between two channel markers. He had written on the chart "no seaway." This was a term used when the passage was so narrow or shallow that a ship had almost no navigational options to turn right or left, so they had to make sure they had engine power to get through the passage. Having no seaway was tricky for a mariner, as it meant once you chose that course you had no real option to turn around or change direction. Having no seaway was not a dire situation, but it was a rough, unpleasant feeling of not having a welcoming harbor to turn into. It seemed to her that their fight was more about not having a commitment to each other to power them through this next hurdle. As she picked the chart off the floor and folded it up, it dawned on her that she had never even moved in with Owen, which had been the plan all along.

Owen drove fast toward the highway. He considered turning back, but he needed gas. He had so much to get done but had a sudden urge to take the whole goddamn day off. As he checked his wallet, there was no money in it. He rummaged around and found a checkbook in his glove compartment. That would have to do. While pumping gas, he spotted Sherry Goodwin's old blue Honda Civic. He smiled at the bumper sticker in back that said, "My other car is a broom."

There was something a bit bewitching about her. She was over by the free air stand, bent over, putting pressure in her tires. Because she was bending over, he could see that her breasts were almost spilling out of her blouse.

She finished filling her tires, and when she turned around to replace the hose, she saw Owen. She flung her long hair back and smiled.

"Heh, Owen," she said, "Where you headin'?"

"I have no idea. You?" He walked closer to her, smiling too.

"Same," she answered. "I am supposed to be looking at a car I might buy. What a day, huh?" It was turning into a beautiful summer day with temperatures in the high seventies.

He nodded and said, "Ayuh. Nothing rarer than a rare day in June."

Seeing her got him to stop rehashing the fight he had just had with Susannah. She was older than Owen and had always run with an even older crowd when they were growing up.

"You in a hurry?" she asked him, as if Owen often had the whole day ahead of him with nothing to do.

"Not really," he said, still staring at her large breasts. "Why?"

"Want to get lunch at the Samoset Inn?" she asked. It was about twenty miles north along the coast. "I can then check out that car I may buy."

"Okay," he agreed.

He went in to pay for the gas while she waited in her car to follow him. As Owen pulled up beside her, they smiled at each other. Their windows were down, sunglasses were on, and the one lane rural highway beckoned.

CHAPTER TWENTY-THREE

Susannah had spent part of the day with Janet, thinking perhaps her relationship with Owen was now over. Janet assured her that, to her knowledge, Dodd men "just go off and sulk somewhere." It was well after a full day of work was done without him that Owen finally returned.

"Where were you?" speaking words that she never wanted to ask a man. She tried to hide the fact that she had been crying. She had also written him a few letters that she was planning to leave for him to read after she had gone. She had thought she would just go that night. She quickly hid those under the bed and forgot about them.

It felt like he was both in the room and miles and miles away. "I tried calling you a bunch of times," she said.

"I needed a day off," he answered. "From everyone."

He offered that he'd spent much of the time just driving around. He'd finally found a place to eat so decided to stay in the area. She noted, "You look like you showered and shaved with industrial soap," as he was cleaner than she had ever seen him. "Are you washing off something here, Owen?" she asked.

"It must have been the rain," he said. "I had a long walk to my car."

His clothes were dry, she noticed. It hadn't rained that day. She was unsure what to accuse him of that she had not done herself. She dropped the subject as best she could. She suggested sitting on the porch. They walked to that favorite room, where they used to sit so often in the beginning. That porch, with its special view of the shipyard, when it was a place just for them—before the rusticators, Kip, Neville and Mysterious Nick, the well-meaning neighbors, the Swiss Misses, Mr. Gregory, reporters, and more. She longed for some of that privacy to return. Perhaps she should have heeded the warnings from Janet's grandmother, who had declared all women who live in a boatyard should never "feed the shipwrights or let them into the house." They don't have relationship manuals for situations like this.

They didn't have too much to say, but sitting beside him, she realized that Owen was dearer to her now, as she did not believe she would have him for much longer.

"Owen?" she said. It was late, and from the porch they could see the ripples of the water and the silhouette of the schooner, getting ever so close to being united with its natural element—the sea.

"Yeah," he answered.

"I think we are in a cult. I think you are the leader of it, and I may well be one of your first disciples."

She could tell that he grasped the irony of it all; it was both humorous and grave.

"You are right," he laughed, seeming less tense. "Only a crazy cult leader like me could get everyone to work for free."

"I think it is more like a tribe than a cult," she added. "At least I thought so when I first came here. I love this tribe if it means my life here in the house, in the boatyard," Susannah said, not sure if there was any point in saying this now. "I have tried to make it like our home."

"I like you being here. I really. . . do. . ." he insisted, although it did not sound that convincing to her.

"Where were you?" she asked again.

"Just driving around," he lied.

"I don't want to break up, Owen. I-I love you," she said, wondering if this was a too little, too late expression of love.

He put his arm around her and hugged her. "Don't go."

They kissed and lingered on the porch for another hour. They eventually made love. Very quietly and formally, but the closeness was there, she thought, and she felt grateful for him.

He lay still for a while and then with a deep breath said, "She'll be named *Spirit of Ossonet*." And he waited for her reaction. "Maybe we will just call her *Spirit*," he said. "The tradition is that a vessel is named after someone's mother, wife, or daughter. I just didn't think it was traditional to name it after my girlfriend."

"Of course," she said, hiding her disappointment but feeling liberated at the same time. "I love the name. It is for everyone."

The following day, Kip could be found quite happily swinging in the small bosun's chair, dangling over the ship twenty feet above ground, not carving "Susannah" into Owen's boat. He was able to see much of the river from his vantage point, and got to enjoy the colors of the surrounding lush green marsh. His time carving the name of the vessel up there in the bosun's chair later became the subject for one of Kip's most sought-after watercolor paintings. He had been feeling very inspired to paint on canvas lately, and he had different scenes already forming in his mind as he hummed along. Meanwhile, Owen was down on the ground pacing, as the launch was set to happen in less than twenty-four hours, and they wanted to get all the scaffolding down off the boat. That meant Kip had to hurry up and finish.

Just past sunset on the night before the launch, Kip called out to everyone, "She's done. Not going to let perfection be the enemy of good!" Mysterious Nick helped him get back on deck. He collected his tools and they clambered down the scaffolding and ramps for the last time.

Everyone paused for a moment to admire Kip's workmanship. He'd carved the name using an old nautical font, added scrollwork under the name and then painted the letters with gold leaf color. It was on both sides of the boat, and the *Spirit of Ossonet* was large and bold enough so that the name of the ship would be easily seen from a passing boat wherever the schooner went. As Kip walked by Owen staring at the name he said, "Don't go changing your mind, now."

"Not likely!" Owen said, and he shook Kip's hand. "Finest kind. Thank you." Owen was proud that beneath the name Kip had added smaller carved lettering naming the builder and the year it was completed. It said, 'Owen Dodd, builder 2018,' as is tradition.

It was time to tear away all the scaffolding surrounding the boat. Owen rang the bell and sent Quinn over to get all the rusticators he could find to help. They came over with industrial lamps from the sheds to work by and steadily removed all ramps, walkways, and access to the schooner. With many hands helping, it took another two hours to clear it all away and the schooner was—for the first time—on full display. With the flood lights it was like opening night with *Spirit of*

Ossonet at center stage, worthy of a standing ovation.

The industrial lights showcased her gorgeous sheer line and shapely curves from stem to stern. Her overall length, including the bowsprit, was sixty-five feet, while from the bottom of the keel to the decks she was twenty feet high. Once her masts were put in, she would be seventy feet in height overall. She weighed about forty-eight tons. She was marvelous to gaze upon—a gorgeous schooner, a remarkable work of folk art, an elegant lady, and a very seaworthy-looking vessel. Considering all the builders and where they all came from, including the Caribbean, *Spirit of Ossonet* was built by the descendants of people and cultures who had been involved in the sea trade in the northern hemisphere for 400-plus years.

Standing behind everyone, Susannah took a photograph of the entire crew looking up and admiring their well-lit masterpiece. She posted her photo on the blog immediately, focusing on the builders and titling it "The true spirits of Ossonet. Launch Day is tomorrow at peak high tide!"

After she posted the picture, she returned to the ship. It was a hot and humid night. Everyone was soaked in sweat. She took off her bandana to wipe the sweat off her face and neck. She was covered with grease, dirt, and specks of paint. Her hair was pulled back, and she now untied it to let all the dust and wood chips fall out of it and brushed it back with her hand. She couldn't help but feel happy in her grime and grit, and even happier when Kip passed her a jug of water. After taking a swig, she missed and got herself wet. Kip took his bandana and handed it to her to wipe herself off. Kip grabbed the water jug and took a swig, saying in a low voice so only Susannah could hear, "We will be heading out of here fairly soon now."

"You are leaving right after the launch?"

"Not quite," he said. "But soon."

She didn't know if he felt the connection they forged on Great Morse Island but she was not going to follow a man somewhere even if she wanted to. Not that he was asking her to.

It was very late, and they all needed some sleep; it would be a big day tomorrow. They were all so tired they simply left the flood lights on. Spirit of Ossonet deserved one more night on land in the spotlight and among her people.

CHAPTER TWENTY-FOUR

It was officially Launch Day and Susannah was up at first light. She stood at the window. The marsh grass had now grown very high and without all the scaffolding and ramps covering it, the schooner looked like it was floating along on a thick, lush sea of green grass. It was more beautiful than a painting, and she rushed out to take a picture.

She walked around the boat to admire every freshly painted, sturdy curve of its planks up close. As she walked towards the far end of the keel, she found Owen kneeling on his haunches placing building blocks around the lower end of the vessel. They were essential as they would be used in part to support the boat as they tried to get it to lean over on its keel edge.

"Owen?" Susannah said. "Are you okay?"

"I don't know if this is going to work," he said. "I am going to be dead soon." He had been saying this a lot lately.

"Can I do anything?" she asked, a bit of his fear rubbing off on her.

"Could you arrange my funeral?"

"Please stop saying that," she said.

"You have to christen the boat before she launches," he told her. "Even if it is flat on its side and I am under it."

"Okay." She wasn't sure if he was joking this time.

"Seb said he will bring champagne for you to use," he said. "Hit the bowsprit hard and say something."

"Okay," she said.

Still on his haunches, looking up at *Spirit* with his hands on his thighs, he was going through the choreography of the day. "The minister's got to ring the church bells when she launches."

"Got it."

"Seb says someone is going to fire a cannon. When he hears that, he will start ringing the bell. Unless I am flattened by the ship. Then we must call an undertaker."

"Better not to ask for whom the bell tolls," Susannah said. "It tolls for thee." Although she was trying to keep it light, hearing her begin his eulogy managed to scare Owen more.

High tide was around 3 p.m., but by midmorning people from around the county were already arriving and starting to set up their lawn chairs. At noon the turnout was way beyond anyone's expectations; people lined the shore, along the town docks, and across the way, wherever they could get a view of the yard.

By near high tide, there were well over two thousand people outside, and it resembled a massive county picnic with chairs, food, beer, umbrellas, and blankets set down on every available open spot, including right under the kitchen window of the house, where Susannah was stationed heating and melting wax. She had been there for the past hour, melting highly flammable paraffin over the stove. The grease and wax were being spread generously all over the railway ties—the track they had built down to the water. The preassigned helpers were bringing the buckets of paraffin, including a tub of Crisco, and spreading it all over the wood and metal rails just like a competitive downhill skier waxes his skis before making a record breaking run. It was hoped that the vessel would also have a gold medal performance down the ways.

The rusticators had set up loudspeakers at the old Gregory shipyard, and they had asked Janet Gregory to be a master of ceremonies, so she had the microphone. Otis Gregory was the honorary guest, and they set him up so he could sit and watch the launch. His eyesight had been failing this past spring and his hearing was worse, but he was a part of it all and was giving a few commands from his chair. He told Janet to speak up into the loudspeaker.

"Owen is calling for wax. They are going to use the wax to grease the ways!" Her father gave her tips on what to say as he was one of the few who had ever seen it done.

The shipwrights were straining to build up a wall of wood blocks and wedges to lean the ship on her side, yet keep her from tipping over while Owen used a very large hydraulic jack to tip it at an even sharper angle. If the lead keel could be coaxed onto its edge, like an ice skater when they are gliding on the edge of their skates, the schooner would be set into motion. There would be very little holding the vessel up, and when—or if—Owen could get the vessel to lean on the very keel edge without toppling, the hope was that the schooner would begin moving from its spot with the help of the grease, catch an edge, and fly down the entire bilgeway and make a big, deep splash. For days, Owen had hoped and prayed that it would move down the greasy, slippery rails and not topple over on its side or get stuck halfway. Once the tide turned and the water level went down, there was no deep water for the boat to plunge into.

Susannah's job right now was in the kitchen, being ordered by Owen to keep heating up the wax. A bunch of helpers was bringing buckets of melted wax back and forth.

They were nearing the moment of peak high tide, and Susannah was going to have to run out and christen the boat. At the same time, she had been told by Owen not to leave the stove unattended. The wax could catch fire.

"No one is smoking in here, I hope," Susannah said to Sherry as she filled her pail with wax. She wasn't sure if Sherry was a smoker.

"I don't smoke. I didn't know Owen smoked a pipe though. I saw him in Islesport the other day. I told him it was bad for his health!" Sherry said.

"Islesport?" Susannah asked. That was about forty miles from Ossonet and it was known for being the location of the Samoset Inn.

"Ouch. That hurt!" Susannah had taken her eye off the wax and was suddenly spattered with boiling wax from its pot on the stove. Sherry was already out the door carrying her pail across the yard. Susannah watched her hand Owen the pail, and he took it with patience and kindness as if she were a luscious milkmaid in a pastoral painting. Susannah strained her neck, watching Sherry and Owen talk, and wondered did she say 'he' or 'we' were in Islesport.

Susannah needed her to come and get more wax. She watched as Sherry walked around as if she were suddenly the lady of the yard, talking to arriving journalists and greeting all their friends while Susannah stirred the vat of wax like some kind of crone.

Just then Quinn rushed in. "Seb said now is the time to go and christen the boat!" Susannah looked out the window, wanting to be out there but unsure what to do about the hot wax. At the same time, one of the local women came inside. She said that the church group had baked a large cake to cut after the launch. It needed to be stored out of the sun.

"Got to have our traditional cake after a schooner launch," she was told, as if this happened every summer instead of once in a lifetime.

Just then Sherry came inside with her pail. Susannah turned off the stove and threw down her oven mitts and took off the heavy apron. "Thank you. Sherry, can you just keep an eye on this wax for a minute? Stove is off but just to be on the safe side."

"What about the cake?" the lady asked. "Is there a cool place for it down cellar?"

The house was so old that the cellar floor was dirt and sometimes at high tide it became flooded. It was no place for a fancy cake.

"I honestly have no idea."

The woman was offended. "Well, it is your party, " she said.

"Sherry, can you help the ladies find a place to store the cake?" Susannah asked. "I need to go christen the boat! Everyone really should be outside now."

Susannah ran off down toward the boat, relieved of her role as the woman of the house. Sherry looked around and cleared off the table in the larger room for the cake and other food the neighbors were bringing out of the hot sun. She opened the door for the neighbors to enter. She was bustling around, enjoying this moment way more than she deserved to. She then dutifully got everyone outside to watch the launch.

Owen spotted Susannah rushing over from his position under the vessel. "Hurry up! Hurry! This thing has got to go soon." Seb had a big magnum of champagne, which he had wrapped in fishnet so the glass would not splinter around her.

There was a short ladder underneath the bowsprit, and she clambered up it as fast as she could. She reached the top. Seb handed her the champagne.

As she raised the bottle, Janet shouted, "They are about to christen the boat!" in her best radio voice.

Susannah stepped up and looked out at the large sea of people waiting for her.

She grasped the bottle with both hands, and honoring traditions, said, "For God and country," and then added, "I christen thee *Spirit of Ossonet!*" She smashed the bottle against the bow and was instantly drenched in champagne. She could taste the refreshing bubbles on her lips, which were already moist from her own salty sweat.

Owen yelled, "Get down! Now! Quick. Quinn. Climb up on deck."

With that, Quinn leapt up the stepladder and grabbed hold of the bowsprit and hoisted himself up and over onto the deck. It was important for someone to be on board with marine rope.

With Quinn on deck, Kip was standing at a distance on a slight hill above the vessel, ready to cut rope tied to a massive chain attached to the ship and to a concrete mooring block on the ground. This would serve as a kind of braking system for the schooner once it got going, so it would not go careening across the basin and smash into the town landing. Once cut, the chain would become as dangerous as a live wire, catching and pulling anything or anyone caught in its wake.

Now alone under the ship, Owen was again lowering the jack so that the vessel leaned enough onto its keel edge to skate down the ramp. It was both urgent and done slowly and was a bit like taking apart a house of cards. Owen looked over at Seb who was standing nearby and silently praying for Owen.

"There is not much holding this boat up right now, Seb."

"And you're under it!" he warned.

The seconds passed as Owen methodically clicked the jack notch by notch so it lowered the vessel onto a razor's edge while the blocks and wedges elevated enough so it would head downhill. Suddenly, as if there were a starting gun, the boat lurched forward. The crowd was nearly motionless as *Spirit* then, thankfully, started off toward the water. The gravity, grease, and momentum, which were the three components to an Ossonet side launch, were working.

"Get out from under there, Owen!" Seb yelled. Owen dropped everything and scrambled out from under the boat as fast as he could.

She was on her way!

"Cut the rope, Kip!" Seb shouted. "Let her go!"

Kip shouted, "Everyone stay clear!" and raised his axe high just behind the concrete weights that would serve as a kind of anchor and brought it down. The chain, attached to the vessel, whipped around like a snake towards the water, dragging the remaining weights with it.

Spirit careened down the bilgeways and over the land's edge with enough speed to plow into the water. At first, it torpedoed into a trough, but it then popped up again bow first like a big fat cork. Sure enough, it started to careen toward the town landing, but the concrete attached to the chain worked and *Spirit* slowed down. Quinn, who had been hanging on out of sight, suddenly jumped up and leaned over the stern with his line. Although the chain and concrete blocks were slowing the boat down, he was ready to toss the rope to waiting hands ready in small skiffs to reign the boat in.

The minute Quinn stood up and could be seen, looking like a cowboy at a rodeo with the big piece of rope in his hand, there was a gasp and then shouts of laughter and cheering from the crowd. Most of the spectators had not known he was there. Shouts of "Huzzah! Huzzah!" came from the shipwrights when seeing Quinn waving from the deck, his long messy hair blowing in the wind which coincided with both cannon fire and the ringing of the church bells. It was pandemonium with everyone hooting, shouting, and clapping. But to the people of Ossonet, Quinn's smiling young face was forever associated with that moment, and often remembered as the face of a new generation of shipbuilders in their town.

Today was also Owen's moment as he alone had risked his life getting under a forty-ton vessel leaning on its side. Everyone rushed over to congratulate him, and as the tension suddenly eased, he had a burst of emotion. Wiping tears away, he slowly collapsed and was lowered gently to the ground. The rusticators propped him up against the barn door, and someone had to help him lift his arm to shake hands. He was spent, and he simply remained there, quite unable to move. As the celebrations continued, the men fed him beer and cake, while many waited to congratulate and talk to him. Susannah eventually reached him and had been told to get him a small cushion for his back. It was the talk of the shipyard that only a few people realized that Owen was pretty much immobile, and his body was in shock. He put on a great party and although he did not move, he never stopped smiling the entire night.

CHAPTER TWENTY-FIVE

The dramatic side launch was the type of near-fiasco-with-a-happy-ending event that caught the attention of news outlets across the country. It turns out that Abby at the *Boston Examiner* had urged the Associated Press writer and photographer to come to the launch. Within hours, the story not only appeared in the *Examiner*, but it was picked up by outlets across the wire. The following day it was listed by *Associated Press* as a top ten news item across the country. Traffic to *Downriver with Dodd* multiplied tenfold when Susannah wrote up a piece for the blog and added lots of great photos taken by many people who were there.

The media attention meant felt like *Spirit* had just won an Academy Award. The morning after the launch, Susannah went to Clydebank and grabbed copies of the *Boston Examiner, USA Today, New York Times, Portland Press Herald* and discovered that many had chosen to put their story on the front page of their newspaper and featured it prominently on social media.

She wanted the men to see the story in print, however—which was still far more important to most rural Mainers than something online. She had all the newspapers in hand, then rustled up all the shipwrights she could find, hungover as they were, to come by for a very special mug up.

Susannah spread the newspapers out on the picnic table, and one by one, the tired, happy, and hungover men poured black coffee, picked up the papers, and slumped down to read in any one of the many lawn chairs people had left behind.

Susannah particularly enjoyed watching Seb as he read the front-page story that featured a photo of him in the *New York Times*. Despite his rough exterior, with his scruffy beard, big, worn hands, work cap, and a busted old pair of bifocals, she thought he looked very serious and dignified—as they all did, quietly reading their own stories.

"It says here you are a genius, Owen," Seb commented as he turned more pages to the end of the long article, carrying even more color photos from the day.

"They say the same in this paper, too, that I am wicked smaht," Owen noted as he had both the *Boston Examiner* and *USA Today* on his lap and the Maine papers beneath them.

Kip picked up the lone Clydebank newspaper, her paper, and smoothed it out on his lap before opening it. In the story, written by Francis Hoyt, he said aloud that Owen Dodd was described as "a national treasure."

"Next stop, the Smithsonian," Neville noted.

After reading the papers, they all stayed seated and simply settled back just to look at *Spirit*. All the painstaking work of framing, planking, then caulking, puttying, and painting her. . .she was watertight and dry. Her masts would go in within a few days, and that would weigh her down deeper in the water, but for now they had a chance to admire all her colors, including the stripe of Oyster White at the waterline. As she gently swayed and tugged at her mooring lines, ripples of water caught the sunlight at different angles, and *Spirit* simply sparkled. One by one they each remarked on her beauty as, like the myth of Narcissus, they could not stop staring at and admiring something of their own creation.

Later, after taking it easy the entire day, Owen went to bed early. Susannah went to the porch and stood at the window where she could see *Spirit* swaying at her mooring. She suddenly remembered that tradition dictated that placing a coin beneath the mast was good luck. The masts would be lowered beneath the deck and attached to the keel very soon. She felt she needed some luck, and it would also ensure safe passage for the schooner.

Susannah had two silver coins from 1925 and 1929 respectively that had belonged to her grandmother at the house. Owen was out cold as she quietly rummaged around in a bureau, put the coins in her pocket, and walked outside. It was a lovely night, so she walked over to the town landing to where she could use the trusty longboat to row out to get a closer look at *Spirit* and place the coins properly where the masts would go in. She had a flashlight with her, and as she reached the high side of the schooner, she realized it would take a feat of acrobatics to get on board. It was impossible. She stood in the rowboat and stretched her hand up to a scupper and tucked the coins into a corner of the deck where she could find them the following day. Both arms were stretched wide to balance herself, but it also gave her a chance to literally hug the vessel. She held it tightly. She rubbed its side like a big animal and briefly rested her head on the freshly painted hull.

As she was returning in the longboat, Kip was watching her come in. He was ankle deep in the muddy water, his wide, long legs and broad shoulders towered in the moonlight. He was waiting to grab a line and help her pull the boat up to shore. He had seen her out on the water from his boat and wanted to make sure she got in okay.

As the boat reached the gravelly bottom, she dropped the oars deftly into the longboat and skillfully strode over the two seats and jumped off the front with the line that she would use to pull the boat in. Kip had been quietly walking towards her to take the line. Instead, she dropped it and put both arms around him in an intimate embrace.

"I don't know, but Owen was with Sherry, I think," she told him.

"I am sorry," he said. "I wish I could help ease your worries, but I am making things worse around here."

She touched his thick hair and asked, "Can I sit with you awhile? Can I say goodbye?"

"Yes," he said. They hauled up the small boat and walked, stealthily, towards his boat and slipped down below into the cabin.

CHAPTER TWENTY-SIX

Not long after the launch, they got the masts stepped and bent the sails on. It was time for the maiden voyage, and it was planned that city officials and a large entourage would later welcome the schooner to her new home in Clydebank, which was about a four hour sail from Ossonet.

The dramatic splashdown of the *Spirit of Ossonet* meant that inquiries had been coming from lifestyle publications, bloggers, newspapers, and a national TV station that had acquired the video from the side launch. It was replayed on the nightly news and shared on social media. For the more intrepid news gatherers, it became something of a watershed moment as the video captured the crowds, the men with their tools and skills, and Owen running from under the schooner while Kip cut the chain, and then Quinn emerging like a young warrior waving to the crowd. People couldn't get enough of the story. Quinn's long hair was even a topic of conversation, and as promised, as soon as the schooner launched, he got a pair of sailcloth scissors, and Susannah photographed him as one of the Swiss Misses, who had returned for the launch, cut it short.

The days before casting off had been something of a media circus and people were clamoring to go on the maiden trip. Instead, they did not let too many people know what day they were leaving and chose to cast off from Ossonet when it was still dark, making it a close-knit crew.

They picked an ideal day for the maiden sail, with the tide high in the morning and an offshore breeze by early afternoon. This would be both a first and last sail for many on the boat. Kip, Neville, Mysterious Nick, and others were leaving Ossonet later that afternoon, with work obligations to fulfill, having had more job offers than ever before.

As the sun came up and they sailed downriver and out toward the open water, a bell began to ring from a large Victorian house on the bluff. The house had a huge wraparound porch, and on the second floor, attached to the house, was a large ship's bell and a rope. They spotted the figure of an older woman in a bathrobe pulling on the long rope, ringing the bell for them as they passed. She waved as they sailed past. They waved back to her.

She continued to ring the bell, and its clear sound that morning stayed with them all whenever they looked back on this day. It was ringing like a fare-thee-well to *Spirit of Ossonet* and the fellowship they had experienced in building her.

About two hours into the sail they were out in the larger bay. Quinn yelled, "Look! Look!"

A humpback whale swam across the front of the bow.

"I think it liked the look of *Spirit*," said Seb, who had been standing near the rail close to Janet. The whale had crossed their bow and then passed them along the starboard side of the boat and given them a good stare with one big eye.

Susannah was sitting next to the wheelhouse while Neville and Kip were watching the trim of the sails. Mysterious Nick was sitting in the stern, smoking a cigarette and looking quite content in his spot. Quinn, with his hair now cut short, had invited one of the Swiss Miss girls along, and they were far forward, sitting near the bowsprit, enjoying the sun, and looking for more whales. There was lots of food and beer, donated mostly by the same locals who had so generously fed them over the long months. It was difficult to muster the usual banter and camaraderie on this quiet day. They were all tired, drained, and bleary-eyed from work, sun, sweat, but mostly the emotional impact of what they had achieved, knowing, too, that for some, their ride on *Spirit* was nearly over.

There was only one captain needed on *Spirit*, and he had not shaved in a few days, letting his beard become stubbly and coarse. While at the wheel of his new ship, he had pulled his cap lower to keep the sun out of his eyes and wore sunglasses. His hair had gotten longer and it was still loose under his cap and blew in the breeze as he drew on his corncob pipe. He stood with one hand on the wheel, one hand on his hip, and one foot up on a deck box. Susannah observed him, and anthropologically speaking, within just a few hours of being at the helm of his schooner, he had transitioned from master shipwright to ship master and commander.

They finally turned toward Clydebank, first passing the outer harbor lined with clapboard houses, then sailing past fishing and lobster boats, getting closer to the long public pier and lively lobster pound that provided outdoor seating. There was a crowd of people awaiting their arrival as they came closer to the pier. Owen gave the crew sharp orders: "Quick! Bow and stern lines to be secured. Sails to be dropped. Lines coiled," he barked. "I said drop sails!" he yelled at Susannah as she and Neville struggled to pull the mast rings down fast enough.

As the Spirit sailed into the dock and the crew tied her lines off, Owen turned toward the crowd. The mayor was there, and of course, Bill King and Francis Hoyt of the *Clydebank News*. They applauded and took photographs as Owen took off his cap and tipped it to the crowd.

After he shook hands with the mayor and other dignitaries, they gave him a bottle of champagne and the first of many citations. The mayor said they were calling it "Owen Dodd Day" in Clydebank. He uncorked the bottle of champagne and took a big gulp and then doused himself and the deck of the schooner with it. The crowd cheered. He made a broad gesture with his arm toward the length and breadth of the vessel and then took another long swig.

Besides Owen, they were all vaguely puzzled by what was unfolding. Janet whispered to Susannah, "It was only a four-hour sail, for chrissakes. We didn't discover land or something." They laughed, but Susannah couldn't help but notice that Owen had not passed the champagne bottle around to her. Owen appeared to by flying solo.

As the gangway opened, all sorts of Clydebankers pushed on to the boat. Susannah watched as the homemade food baskets from the Ossonet families were consumed by the Clydebankers who grabbed all the sandwiches, cold beer, and gobbled up Owen's mother's homemade brownies. Her own editor, Bill, was among them, eating what looked like homemade meat pie from her Ossonet neighbor. He asked Susannah to get him a napkin as it was out of his reach. As she handed it to him, she looked over at Mysterious Nick, who seemed to have taken an instant dislike to all the Clydebankers. He stood apart, smoking his cigarette and looking restless. Susannah walked up to him and said, "That cigarette looks good enough to eat." He handed it to her, and she took a long drag. She blew the smoke out in such a way that it inadvertently got into Owen's face as he walked past. Owen waved the smoke away and gave her a curious, stern look as she never smoked. Nick seemed to get a kick out of it.

Owen had a ship's bell near his wheel, and he rang it to get everyone's attention. He thanked them, but especially all the crew and the support from his town. He introduced them all and thoughtfully congratulated Janet Gregory, who had won a seat on the Ossonet Board of Selectmen. He encouraged everyone from the county to support her efforts to pass a new bylaw that would make it difficult to build a marina off the Dodd property, at least for a while. He momentarily got choked up as he looked around.

"Until we get another ship to build," he announced, "and I pray that will be within my lifetime, we are launching a tour boat company and will be offering sailing trips on the *Spirit of Ossonet* out of this pier right here. Make sure to sign up for our next charter!"

Susannah had suspected— but was not sure— he really was going to go into selling tickets for two-hour sails. He nudged her soon after his announcement and said, "I promise to keep you busy while you keep working at the paper." It was all decided. She had now officially landed herself—again—into the life of a man on a mission. Ironically, she had recently received an email from Eric Strand in England. He had seen the article about the launch of *Spirit* in an international newspaper.

"Congratulations, dear Susannah," he wrote. "Your keen skills at observation and study made you a promising anthropologist then, and now your chronicles of life in a provincial Maine town have put you at the head of the class once again. Wishing you all the best, yours truly, etc."

The long sail to Clydebank and the reception were ending. The rusticators had driven over with a couple of cars to take them all back to Ossonet. One by one they piled in. Susannah stayed on with Owen until it got late. He said he thought he might sleep on the boat that night just to keep an eye on it.

When she got back to the house, Kip, Neville, and Mysterious

Nick had left her some flowers in a vase and a trunnel with all their names written on it. Before they parted, Kip gave Owen one of his paintings. It was a watercolor of *Spirit* in the marsh grass on the morning of her launch. Everything was still and calm and vibrant just before she was catapulted into the water. Kip had perfectly captured the moment with his fine brush. In fact, he had been painting and selling his art again, and after he left he would send them a photo or text and tell them where he was selling his art and how great that was going. Neville went home to St. Vincent for a visit, after sailing with Mysterious Nick and Kip to Great Morse Island on Kip's boat.

On the land line, there was a message, and it was a call from Claire MacInnis. She was congratulating Owen on the launch of the Spirit.

Claire then said, "But I am calling to leave this message for Susannah, too." Susannah called her back. It turns out that she was waiting to hear about a large grant from the state of Maine for women-owned businesses. Claire said that if she got the grant, she wanted to work with Susannah on marketing and new business development. "I could hire you on the spot then," she said.

Susannah was also surprised to learn that Kip had recently been in touch with Claire as she went on to say, "We are also excited about our boat building project for Kip. I am glad to hear he won't be going back to New York City right away, and we may be able to keep him in Maine a bit longer." Susannah hadn't realized Kip might be staying on in Maine as he had mentioned that some of his New York gallery owners were anxious to get him to the city to display his Ossonet paintings.

CHAPTER TWENTY-SEVEN

As the summer weather set in, Owen was right; there did seem to be a demand for sails around the coast off Clydebank. Despite how well they did with digital marketing techniques, Owen insisted the best way to sell tickets was by using a sandwich board and walking up and down the streets before each sail. Sales were quite brisk and tickets were sold using mostly cash. Delighted, Owen would go below and stuff the cash into various seams between the planks as he had not yet gotten a cash box. He would lightly tap the cash into the seam with a caulking mallet as a temporary cash box and stay on the boat more often at night 'for security purposes.' At the end of each sail, he put out a bucket and the passengers would give him cash tips. That also got stuffed into places down below. Extracting payment for the hours she worked on board was simple as she would pull her share of the cash out of the seams. He never kept track. Susannah scolded him as he often left the boat to run errands with wads of cash down below.

By late August, Owen and Susannah had spent at least fifty days sailing around Clydebank and the coast, earning money along the way. Because of the hot summer nights, Owen said he much preferred sleeping on the boat. Susannah found the bunks to be uncomfortably narrow so often stayed at her apartment or at his house. When they weren't busy with a paying charter, friends often came along for a free sail, and the shipbuilders and rusticators had a lifelong invitation to sail anytime. Everyone was amused by Owen's business model and acumen, and it was quite a show as he had also begun to dress like a pirate to attract and entertain customers. He wanted Susannah to dress in a costume too. He thought cleavage was going to help sell tickets, and plumping up her breasts with a blousy top and corset did draw attention to the sign for ticket sales and the boat. During the sails Owen also felt it was his duty to explain and illustrate how schooners and sailing ships are more regimented and follow a chain of command. He also liked to explain to passengers the whole story of how the schooner was built and praised the team that built her. He missed them.

As far as what would happen once the fall weather came, Owen insisted that he would keep tinkering in the barn until a hoped-for schooner job came along. He said he would rather just tinker than work for someone else. He assumed Susannah would keep working at the *Clydebank News* and it was, once again, going to be a busy season for sewage treatment and road closures.

It was a mid-September weekend and Owen was sailing. Susannah had received two messages on her cell phone, one from Claire MacInnis telling her that the funding came through from the state of Maine and she could hire Susannah if she were interested. The other message was from Kip. He had called just to say "Hello to *Spirit* and all of you!"

There was a knock at the door. "Anyone home?" It was Janet Gregory. Janet had been working hard at her new role as selectwoman and it seemed to suit her. She had helped address the bylaw that preserved the waterway around the town landing for shipbuilding and most of the people in town agreed to keep it in place for now. She and Seb had both taken on more leadership roles in the town. It was hoped one day Owen would get another schooner to build, and it seemed that Owen had the full support of the town now. He was also a bit of a celebrity wherever he went up and down the coast. Janet knew he was spending a lot of nights on the boat in Clydebank. So, unbeknownst to Susannah, she had been keeping tabs on Owen a bit over the summer.

"So, you guys had a good sail late last night?" Janet asked gingerly as she walked into the kitchen where Susannah offered her some coffee. They went onto the porch and sat down together.

"I was in Clydebank last night, and I saw you out for an evening sail. Just the two of you," Janet said. "It looked like a beautiful night."

Susannah's expression gave Janet a moment of doubt.

Janet said softly. "That was you, right?"

"That wasn't me," Susannah answered. She knew her voice

sounded cold, but she was also relieved that her own doubts were justified. "I was covering a planning board meeting for the paper and then came here. "

"Oh." Janet was at a loss for words. "Shit."

"Do you think it was Sherry?" Susannah asked. Janet considered the vague silhouette she had seen from shore of two people sitting very close together, sailing along blissfully under the full moon.

"I could not tell who it was," she said truthfully.

The women sat quietly for a while. Susannah made sure not to shoot the messenger and get angry at her friend.

"I got a job offer today, Janet," Susannah finally said. "It's with that female shipyard owner, Claire MacInnis."

"I think you should go for it." Janet said.

"Janet," Susannah said, as they exchanged hugs, "thank you for telling me about what you saw. I won't say a word about it right now but I will always never love you."

"I will never love you either," Janet said. "It has been quite a time around here."

The following day, they had about ten paying passengers for the afternoon sail. Captain Owen, who had stayed on board the night before, was instructing a passenger on how to tack the boat. Susannah went to the passenger's aid, as it was a cumbersome task, and they needed more hands to help.

"Get the boom around," he commanded. "Susannah. No. All the way around! Walk it across the deck! Now. Hurry up!" He was tacking up and down the harbor to get out to the open water, so each time he had Susannah pushing the sail from one side of the boat to the other. The wind was so light they had barely made it past the town beach.

"Walk it. Push it out from the edge. We've got to get the boat around!" Owen demanded.

Susannah pushed the boom across the deck and then out toward the open water so the wind would fill the sail.

"Push it farther!" Owen shouted.

He was still commanding her to push the boom far out so that the bit of breeze would fill the large, flapping sail. She pushed it out as far as she could reach and then she climbed up onto the rail of the boat and hung onto the boom. A strong puff of wind suddenly filled the sail while she was holding on to the boom and it simply carried her out over the water. Susannah had gone beyond the reach of the railing and had run out of boat. All she could do was hang on. The sail filled beautifully. As the boat started to turn and move out towards the open water, Susannah had no choice but to let go and drop into the water below.

They were close to shore, and the water was quite warm. People on board were concerned, but as Susannah ripped off the heavy portions of her pirate wench costume she gave them a thumbs up. Owen watched her as he steered, both frustrated and bemused. One of the rusticators was on board that day and stepped in to fill her position. He gave her a send-off wave. Her shift was done and *Spirit* sailed away from her.

She got to shore and caught a lift back to her apartment and packed it up. She then went to the Dodd house and retrieved most of her things. She drove out of Ossonet on the same road that had brought her there by chance over one year ago. She headed north and stopped to look back down the peninsula from the highest part of the road. She thought she spotted a white sail on the horizon that looked like *Spirit of Ossonet*. She smiled, and wiping tears away, flipped a coin and kept going. She would be able to find her way with the set of tools she had with her all along